CAN TRUE LOVE
SURVIVE
HIGH SCHOOL?

a **DATING GAME** novel by Natalie Standiford

LITTLE, BROWN AND COMPANY

New York ⁓ Boston

First Edition: August 2005

Little, Brown and Company
Time Warner Book Group
1271 Avenue of the Americas, New York, NY 10020
Visit our Web site at www.lb-teens.com

The characters and events in this book are fictitious. Any similarity to real
persons, living or dead, is coincidental and not intended by the author.

Cover photos from top left, © Digital Vision Photography/Veer, © Michelle
Pedone/Photonica, © PicturePress/Photonica, © Photodisc Red/Getty
Images, © Betsie Van Der Meer/Photonica, © Emma Innocenti/Photonica,
© Brand X Pictures/Getty Images, © Tony Anderson/Iconica, © Mario
Lalich/Photonica.

Interior created and produced by Parachute Publishing, L.L.C.
156 Fifth Avenue
New York, NY 10010

ISBN: 0-316-11042-6

10 9 8 7 6 5 4 3 2 1

CWO

Printed in the United States of America

For the two Kathleens—Nixon and Clare—and all the Natalies: Natalie Rebecca, Natalie Elizabeth, Elizabeth Natalie, Natalie Zofia, and Natalie Jane.

1 Never Been Kissed

To:	hollygolitely
From:	your daily horoscope

HERE IS TODAY'S HOROSCOPE: CAPRICORN: Whatever little scheme you're cooking up in that brain of yours—forget it! I'm telling you, it's going to blow up in your face. Are you listening to me? Hello?

To: hollygolitely
From: piedpiper
Re: come visit?
Hollster,
Heads up—sterling quad's spring blowout is three weeks
away. why don't you haul your busty little self up here
for it? I'm sure curt and jen won't stop you. it's a huge

party all weekend. You haven't visited me once yet and my freshman year is almost over! bring mads and lina if you want (if their jailers will let them out). I miss having you around to make me feel superior.

Love, the pipester

Holly Anderson forwarded the e-mail to her best friends, Lina Ozu and Madison Markowitz. The Pipester, aka Holly's older sister, Piper, was a freshman at Stanford University. Holly would have visited her at school a long time ago—Palo Alto was only about an hour and a half away from home—but Piper had never invited her before. Typical of Piper to make it seem like Holly had neglected her, rather than the other way around.

Ding! An instant message. Mads had already gotten the e-mail.

mad4u: I'm there! But I have to ask m.c. and the overlord first. Piper is right when she calls them jailers. Free the carlton bay two!

By that she meant herself and Lina, the only two fifteen-year-olds in Carlton Bay, California who weren't allowed to do whatever they wanted, whenever they wanted. According to Mads, anyway. Holly's parents,

Curt and Jen, were more permissive.

> **hollygolitely:** bet your parents will give in if lina's say yes.

Another IM came in, this time from Lina.

> **linaonme:** I already asked sylvia. She said we'll see. Should have gone straight to dad.
>
> **mad4u:** we have to go! krazy kollege weekend! I'll die if I miss it!
>
> **hollygolitely:** you've got 3 weeks to find a way.
>
> **mad4u:** I'll find a way. Btw, have u seen those ads for kiss me stinky? I want 2 c it so bad!
>
> **linaonme:** starring liam price! Yum!
>
> **hollygolitely:** me 2. Let's go 2gether. It's too chick-flicky for rob.
>
> **mad4u:** stephen too. Also 2 dopey for him.

Kiss Me, Stinky was a new movie that had just opened at the Carlton Bay Twin. Rob Safran, a hunky swimmer, was Holly's boyfriend and Mads had just started seeing the brainy, serious Stephen Costello. Lina didn't have a boyfriend. She was in love with Dan Shulman, their Interpersonal Human Development teacher. Maybe if Liam Price, the latest teen heartthrob, went to their school she'd forget about Dan. But Holly doubted it. To

Lina, Dan was almost as unattainable as a movie star, but that didn't stop her from building her world around him.

> hollygolitely: ok, we'll all go together. Deal?
>
> mad4u: deal.
>
> linaonme: deal. What's up 2nite?
>
> mad4u: homework.
>
> hollygolitely: fowlers coming over for drinks. With britta. I'm going 2 try 2 find a boy 2 match her with.
>
> linaonme: good luck. R u sure she likes boys?
>
> hollygolitely: pretty sure. I think she prefers amoeba, tho.

"Britta has just *struggled* with Calculus this year," Peggy Fowler said. "Haven't you, honey? I think she got an A-minus on the last test."

"An A-minus doesn't cut it at Harvard," Gordon Fowler said.

Holly sipped her iced tea and smiled and nodded at the Fowlers. They were sitting in front of the big stone fireplace, now filled with vines and flowers for spring, in the great room of the Andersons' comfortable contemporary house. Eugenia Anderson, Holly's mother, had put out some cheese and olives and vegetables to have with cocktails. She wore her favorite long, red, embroidered caftan with flat gold slippers, her straight dark hair chopped at her pointy chin. Holly's father, Curtis—dressed in his usual expensive golfwear, his round, ruddy face hearty with cocktail camaraderie—shook martinis. Holly sat on the couch, bare feet tucked under her, in jeans and a t-shirt. She didn't see any reason to get dressed up for the Fowlers.

Across the coffee table from her, the Fowlers sat lined up in a row, Papa Bear, Mama Bear and Baby Bear. Baby Bear, or Britta, a junior at the Rosewood School for Alternative Gifted Education (RSAGE), where Holly was a sophomore, was almost as tall as her father. She had his big bones and abundant curly brown hair, her mother's large brown eyes, and a reticent, shy manner that wasn't much like either of them. She wore small, silver-rimmed glasses and a long-sleeved flowery dress. Holly would have bet cash money that Britta's mother had picked it out for her.

"I don't want to go to Harvard anyway," Britta said.

"Oh, that's right," Peggy said. "You want to go to *Stanford*." She pronounced "Stanford" as if someone had offered her a dirty diaper with her drink. "With all the jocks." Then she glanced at the Andersons, remembering that Piper, their older daughter, was a freshman at Stanford. "Don't get me wrong, it's a *great* school. I just don't think it's the best place for Britta."

"They have a good microbiology department," Britta said.

"What if you get into Harvard?" Gordon said. "Or Yale? Are you telling me you'd turn them down for Stanford?"

Holly sucked a slice of lemon out of her glass and gnawed on the rind. If she had to sit there and listen to another minute of this she'd scream. She was looking forward to college as much as anyone, but the Fowlers were so obsessed. . . . Poor Britta, Holly thought. She really needs help. Why didn't Jen jump in with some kind of trivial social news? That was her specialty, and she normally didn't let dull conversations drag on this long without interruption.

"I worry about Britta," Peggy went on, as if Britta wasn't sitting right next to her. "Do you know she's never been out on a date, not once? Ever? And look what a pretty thing she is." She lifted one of Britta's curls as proof of her prettiness. *And she is pretty*, Holly thought. *Or she could be, if she loosened up a little. But how is she supposed to do that with her parents on her back every second?*

"It's a shame, really," Peggy said. "Holly, how old are you now?"

"Sixteen," Holly said.

"Sixteen," Peggy said. "So she must have been out on at least one date by now, hasn't she, Jen?"

Jen cast a cool glance at Holly. "Ha! One date! The girl's been a boy-trap since she was twelve."

"Hello? I'm sitting right here," Holly snapped.

"Just look at her!" Jen added.

Everyone stared at Holly, judging her boy-trapping qualities. She had long, wavy blond hair and a full red mouth, but Holly knew what Jen was really referring to when she called her a boy-trap. Her breasts, which were a little on the big side. Okay, a lot on the big side. They used to embarrass Holly, but now she wasn't bothered by them—except when someone *very rudely* drew attention to them. Her own mother, of all people, should know better by now.

"She's a looker, no doubt about it," Gordon said.

Holly officially wanted to die. Or kill her mother. Or both. Usually Jen was more of social smoothie than this. She must have had a little too much wine already.

"Well, I don't see why Britta shouldn't have a boyfriend, too," Peggy said. "It's part of high school. She's only got one more year left. As long as it doesn't affect her grades or any of her other activities." She stared at her daughter, thinking this over, still playing with Britta's hair. "It's not that boys don't like her. I think she's afraid."

Britta pushed her mother's hand away from her face. "I'm not afraid. Do we have to sit here and talk about this in front of everyone? It's none of their business. And it's none of yours, either."

The room went silent. Holly was afraid to move anything but her eyes, which darted from Britta to Peggy to Gordon to Curt to Jen. Everyone was frozen in an awkward moment. Somebody do something!

"Peggy, remember Martha Bray, that skinny girl from St. Elizabeth's?" Good old Jen, right on time. She and Peggy had gone to a fancy Catholic boarding school together. "I saw her name in the paper the other day. She and her husband own a vineyard up in Napa."

"Martha Bray?" Peggy tried to remember. "X-Ray Bray?"

While they yammered away about prep schoolmates and the men mixed more drinks, Holly nodded at Britta. "You don't really want to sit here and listen to this, do you? Let's go up to my room."

Holly had to agree with the Fowlers on one point—Britta needed something to get her out of that house and away from them. And a boyfriend was just the ticket.

"My parents are unbelievable pains," Britta said.

"And mine aren't?" Holly said. "Britta, you need to relax. You need some distraction from all the pressure you're under."

"Sometimes I think so, too," Britta said. "But who has the time?" When she wasn't doing schoolwork she was padding her college transcript with activities like basketball, internships at hospitals and laboratories, volunteer work at a nursing home, violin lessons. Experience with boys would not help her get into college, Holly knew. But college was just four years of your life. It wasn't everything. And anyway, didn't they say it was good to be well-rounded?

"You make time." Holly sat down at her computer and logged onto The Dating Game, a Web log that she and Lina and Mads had started. It began as a school project, a survey of the sexual attitudes of their fellow students, and morphed into a matchmaking site with personal ads, quizzes, questionnaires, and an advice column.

"Want to fill out one of the matchmaking question-naires?" Holly asked. "Just for fun?"

Before Britta had a chance to answer, Holly filled in her name, age, and other vital information. "Gender . . . grade . . . Are you a virgin?" Holly assumed the answer was yes.

"Okay," Holly said. She pulled up an extra chair and patted the seat. Britta obediently sat down. "Have you kissed someone of the opposite sex?"

"No," Britta said.

Holly's head wanted to shake in disapproval, but she checked it. Seventeen years old and never even kissed a boy! This was an extreme case. "I guess I can skip these," she said, pointing to the questions about going to second base, third base, and so on. Next came the inkblot test. Holly showed Britta a symmetrical black blob and said, "What's the first word or image that comes into your mind when you look at this?"

Britta peered at the blot. "A poorly dissected frog."

"O-kay. What are your dating requirements: Cuteness? Brains?"

Britta suddenly looked horrified. "You're not going to fix me up with someone, are you?"

"Of course. What did you think we were doing?"

"I'm not ready," Britta said. "I don't want to go out with some strange boy I don't even—"

"Relax. We'll deal with that part when we get there. Now just answer the question. Hypothetically. If you went out with a boy, what would you want him to be like? It's a perfectly reasonable question."

"Okay." Britta stared at the screen. "Brains, definitely. Sense of humor is nice. A good heart. I don't care about money or athletic ability or music. Honesty, yes."

"And looks?" Holly asked.

"Well . . . yes. Okay. Looks are good. And a sense of responsibility."

"Any dealbreakers?" Holly asked, going over the list. Britta chose drugs and bad skin.

"Now," Holly said. "Let's go through some boys' questionnaires and see if there's anyone you like."

They scrolled through the boys who had signed on to the site looking for matches. Britta found something wrong with every one of them.

"Too stupid—I know, he's in my French class. Too dull. Too full of himself—you can tell from the picture . . ."

"Girls!" Jen called up the stairs. "The Fowlers are ready to leave!"

Britta stood up, shrugging. "Oh well."

"You're not getting off that easily," Holly said. "Don't worry, I'll find somebody good for you. You can't tell everything from these questionnaires, you know. You've got to take a chance and meet a person face-to-face."

"It's just—I don't know," Britta said. "What if I really like someone and he doesn't like me back? I don't think I could stand it."

"It can be rough," Holly said. "But it's worth the risk. Don't worry, Britta—someone will like you a lot. I know it."

# 2 El Diario

HERE IS TODAY'S HOROSCOPE: VIRGO: You think you're getting away with something. You will find out later that it got away with you.

El Diario del Dating Game by Madison Markowitz
(a new diary feature on the Dating Game Web log!)
(Yes, I'm ripping off Nuclear Autumn. So what? Is she the only person in the world allowed to have an online diary?)

Autumn Nelson was in Mads' class. She detailed every moment of her life on a popular blog called "Nuclear Autumn."

I have a few things to get off my scrawny chest. Like this: LITTLE SISTERS SUCK. *Mine, let's call her "Audrey," is probably the most annoying creature who ever lived. You don't need to know the gory details (involving a brand-new pair of boots chewed to smithereens because a certain eleven-year-old spawn of Satan let our puppy loose in my room . . . Sure, she claims it was an accident, but no one who knows Her Satanic Majesty could doubt that she did it 100 percent on purpose)— let's just say Audrey and I have been fighting a lot lately. It upsets M.C. (my mother). I think it upsets the Dark Overlord (my father) too, but he's so spaced out and in his own world it's hard to tell. M.C. wants it to stop. She has actually threatened to send me and Audrey to a couples counselor to work out our problems! But now there's a new threat—and this one is even worse.*

My mother has written a play. It's based on her life from birth to age twenty-two, and it's the stupidest play ever. It's called Touched: The Story of a Sensitive Girl. *Is that not vomitous? I wouldn't care, except that the Carlton Bay Playhouse has actually agreed to stage it. Yes, in a theater. In public. To a paying audience!*

(It's a very small theater, and they have a new director, and M.C. says they're going experimental. Is "experimental" a euphemism for "crazy?")

Audrey wants to be in the play, and M.C. wants me to

be in it, too. I'd have to play my own mother at the turning point of her life: the moment she discovered, at age 13, that she has ESP.

Yes, M.C. has ESP. Or she used to; she says her power has faded with age. It's a terrible skill for a mother to have even a little of, when you're her daughter. She always kind of knows what you're thinking, or she thinks she does, which is almost as bad.

Anyway, M.C. is not usually so bossy, but being a playwright is her lifelong dream, and it's making her insane. (She's a pet therapist in real life. I thought that was her lifelong dream, but she keeps changing it.) I don't mind the idea of acting in a play. But I won't stand on a stage and speak lines like this:

"Oh, Papa, Mama, don't you see? I'm having such a strange feeling, like something's vibrating in my head. I'm getting a message . . . The telephone is about to ring. It's going to be the plumber . . . yes, the plumber. He can't come until tomorrow!"

The phone rings a few minutes later, and the plumber says he won't be able to fix the clogged sink until the next day. My character and her parents are stunned at my psychic abilities.

I refuse to audition for the part. M.C. can't make me. And that is my final word on the matter.

To get off the subject of me for a minute, I would like to

ask my readers out there a question: Did anybody besides me see the way Rebecca dissed Autumn at lunch this afternoon? She nearly spat in Autumn's face when she tried to sit down at their usual table. Are they having a fight? What about? If you know, e-mail me. Not that I care.

This is Madison Markowitz, over and out.

"She's thinking, 'If I talk on my cell while I wander around aimlessly with nothing to do, everyone will think I have a life,'" Mads said. She and Stephen were sitting on a bench at the marina on Sunday afternoon, watching the people stroll by and playing a game Stephen made up called "What Are They Thinking?" At that moment a platinum-haired girl walked slowly past a group of boys, chattering and laughing into her cell phone. Mads was convinced that she was pretending to be talking to some very witty friend for the boys' benefit.

"She's fake laughing," Mads said. "Look. She's saying, 'You want to fly me to Hawaii in your private jet? But Hunter, I already have a date tonight.'"

"And the boys are thinking, 'Why is that girl walking so slowly? Does she think she's hot because she has a cell phone?'" Stephen said.

"Oh look! Now she's thinking, 'I hope no one noticed me picking my thong strap out of my butt,'" Mads said.

"But someone did notice," Stephen said. "Eagle-eye Mads."

Mads laughed. Stephen had a way of liking everything he saw in Mads—even the things she didn't like herself. It made her feel good.

"What about that guy?" Stephen asked, pointing at a thirty-something man with a thatch of blond hair so stiff and perfectly coifed it looked like it had hairspray in it. Mads had never seen someone walk so stiffly, with such ramrod posture.

"He's thinking, 'If I don't move my head, my hair will stay perfect,'" Mads said.

"Yeah," Stephen said. "'But if one single strand comes loose, I'll never be able to show my face in public again!'"

Mads leaned against Stephen and he put his arm around her. She really liked him. She wished she could spend more time with him, but he was a junior and she was a sophomore, and they had no classes together. And most days after school he helped his mother in her studio. She was a sculptor and Stephen did apprentice work for her, cutting pieces of metal and wood to her precise specifications, welding, hauling things around, stuff like that.

A good-looking couple strolled by, hand-in-hand. At the sight of them, Mads' breath caught in her throat. The boy was lean and broad-shouldered with longish, shaggy blond hair and a handsome face made somehow handsomer by a slightly too-big nose. The girl was blond, too, with straight hair and bangs and slender legs. The two of them had a golden aura of cool around them. They stood out.

The girl, as Mads knew, was Jane Cotham, nineteen, a part-time student at Geddison, a local college. The boy was Sean Herman Benedetto, senior at RSAGE, star swimmer, and the monster crush, if not the love, of Mads' life.

Stephen nodded at Sean and said, "He's thinking, 'I wonder if my glutes look good in these jeans?'"

"Heh, yeah," Mads said, half-laughing. She was zoned out, staring at Sean. He had that effect on her. And she couldn't help thinking that his glutes *did* look good in his jeans. He gave Jane's hand a little tug, pulling her closer to him so he could wrap his arm around her. He was so into her. Anyone could see it.

And Jane is probably thinking, "I'm the luckiest girl in town," Mads thought, but she didn't say it out loud. It was a good thing Stephen couldn't read *her* thoughts. She liked him a lot, but Sean . . . he was, like, on another level.

They disappeared into a shop, and the spell was broken. Mads leaned happily against Stephen's thin arm. He was cool in his own way, so smart but not snobby. Mads could be flighty but Stephen saw through it. He found the sense in her nuttiness.

"Too bad you don't have ESP like your mom," Stephen said. "Then you could *really* read people's minds."

"Oh god, don't remind me." Mads dropped her head on his shoulder. She knew what awaited her when she got home. That stupid play. Her mother, M.C., had been campaigning hard for Mads to audition for the part of "Teen Mariah" all week. Audrey already had all of "Little Mariah's" lines memorized.

"Maybe it won't be so bad." Stephen got up and pulled Mads to her feet. It was nearly dinnertime, time to go home. "It might be fun to be in a play."

"Stephen, you don't know what this play is like. It's not exactly Eugene O'Neill. It's not even *Cats*."

"Poor Mads, the reluctant actress." His arm around her, he pulled her toward his car, a red Mini Cooper. "Just tell your mother you don't want to do it. Say you're too busy with school or something."

"I've tried!" Mads said. "I've begged and pleaded and cried. I've threatened to run away and join a cult. She doesn't care. She thinks Audrey and I will learn to get along better if we're in this play together. And it's her dream to see her daughters playing her on stage. She's on some kind of wack ego trip."

"Sounds like it." They got into the car and drove through the narrow streets of Carlton Bay, a small, pretty waterfront town that stretched across a row of gentle hills to a green valley. Stephen dropped her off at her house. "See you at school tomorrow. Hope so, anyway." She turned toward him. He pulled her close and gave her a long, slow kiss. She wrapped her arms around his neck. Any lingering thoughts of Sean disappeared like soap bubbles. Her first real boyfriend! It was better than a daydream.

The warm feeling Stephen gave her dissipated as soon as she opened the front door to her house. "Oh, Mama, I can't live on a farm in Minnesota forever," Audrey recited, quoting one of her lines from the play. "I must be near the ocean. I have to see the sea before I die!"

As a girl, M.C. had been Mary Claire Olmsted, third child of Minnesota dairy farmers. The play was about her childhood and her rebellious decision to leave the farm at seventeen to go to college at Berkeley in California and be a hippie.

Instead of her usual Bratz Doll/Britney-on-tour wear, Audrey was dressed in her best approximation of a Minnesota farm girl's outfit: white puffy-sleeved blouse, red gingham jumper, hair in two strawberry-blond braids. On her feet were a pair of shiny red shoes. Typical Audrey to have such a Hollywood-fake vision of Minnesota.

"Who are you supposed to be, Dorothy in *The Wizard of Oz?*" Mads said.

19

"I'm trying to stay in character as much as possible before my audition," Audrey said. "Haven't you ever heard of Stanislavsky's Method of Acting, you ignoramus?"

"Cram it," Mads muttered, brushing past Audrey and hoping to escape into her room. Where did she get that Stanislavsky stuff? She was usually more Powerpuff Girl than Russian intellectual.

"Girls, dinner's ready," M.C. called from the kitchen. Mads veered right and headed for the kitchen. Good thing she was hungry, because she couldn't think of another good reason to suffer through a meal with these people.

Her father, Russell, pulled a tray of whole wheat biscuits out of the oven. M.C. set a hot vegetable-and-cheese casserole on the table. "Ho, Madison!" Russell cried in his jolly voice, nabbing Mads on her way to her seat and kissing the top of her head.

"Hi, Dad." Her father was the only sensible person in the family. Or maybe he just seemed that way because he generally kept his mouth shut while his wife and daughters expressed every thought that popped into their heads.

Audrey sat down. M.C. poured them ice water.

"Papa, please pass the corn and them sweet, sweet tomaters," Audrey said in a fake hick voice. She and Mads never called their parents "Papa" or "Mama." That came from the play.

"You don't have to be in character all the time, you know, Audrey," Russell said. "We're out of corn and tomaters. Have some ratatouille. It's got cheese in it."

"And anyway, I never talked like that," M.C. said. "I certainly never said 'tomaters.'"

"I'm doing the Method!" Audrey snapped. "I have to become Little Mariah—*my* version of her. You people have no respect for the way an artist works."

"Artist?" Mads said. "You mean a big fat slice of ham! Oink oink!"

"Mama! Papa! That young 'un is picking on me!"

"Don't tease her, Mads," Russell said, but the twinkle in his eye told her he was on her side.

"I appreciate your enthusiasm for my play, Audrey," M.C. said. "I wish Madison could muster up a little more interest."

Mads scowled and took a bite of ratatouille. It was scalding hot. She spit it back out on her plate and reached for her water glass.

"Mads can't act," Audrey said.

"I could if I wanted to," Mads said. "I just don't want to at this time."

"I think you'd be wonderful," M.C. said. "If you'd just try out for the part, I know you'd catch the acting bug. What harm could it do?"

"It's embarrassing," Mads said. "I don't want to do it."

"I wish you'd at least try," M.C. said.

"No."

M.C. frowned. "I don't like this new attitude of yours, Madison. You never used to be so stubborn!"

"Honey, don't push her," Russell said.

"It's just—she's being so unreasonable!" M.C. cried. Her blue eyes were moist behind her red cat's-eye glasses. "It's the very first production of my very first play. I'd think she'd be proud of it! All I'm asking is that she try out. That's all."

Mads felt bad. She knew this play meant a lot to her mother. And she'd be happy to go to opening night and clap louder than anybody. But why did she have to act in it?

"Don't cry, Mama," Audrey said in a twang that was more Alabama than Minnesota. "Don't you see? The sun will rise again tomorrow, same as today, same as always . . ."

"Mom, I just don't see what the big deal is," Mads said. "Audrey will be in the play. Isn't that enough?"

"All I'm asking you to do is try out." It wasn't like M.C. to be this fixed on something. But the play meant so much to her, and the harder she pushed, the more Mads resisted. She couldn't help it; it was like a reflex.

"No."

"Madison, I insist you audition for the play. If you don't get the part, fine. But you must at least try out . . . or I won't let you go to Stanford with Holly and Lina."

"What?!?" Mads was outraged. "This is blackmail!"

"Honey, do you think that's fair?" Russell said.

"It's just an audition," M.C. said. "It's not that much to ask."

"I don't believe this!" Mads cried. "Dad! Pull your Dark Overlord thing and overrule her!"

Russell glanced from his daughter to his wife. "It means a lot to her, Mads. It won't kill you to try out. I mean, it's not as if you've got crippling shyness or anything."

Mads let her fork clatter against her plate. It was so unfair! But when she weighed the two choices, M.C. won. There was no way Mads was going to miss the Crazy College Weekend. Even if she had to get on a stage and completely humiliate herself. She'd been embarrassed before and lived; she could survive it again.

"All right," Mads said. "You win. I'll audition. But that means I definitely get to go to Stanford, right?"

"Yes," M.C. said.

"Actually, honey, I thought we were going to discuss that tonight," Russell said.

M.C. shot him a sharp look. Matter settled.

"Guess not," Russell said.

"Mom, don't make her audition," Audrey whined. "She'll ruin everything."

"That's enough, Audrey," M.C. said. "It's a chance for you two to learn to get along. Would you rather go to couples therapy?"

"She'll suck!" Audrey said.

"I thought you were staying in character," Mads said.

Audrey pushed away from the table. "I'll be in my dressing room." She went upstairs.

"Audrey!" M.C. called. "Come back and finish your ratatouille!"

"I'll go get her." Russell wearily got up from the table.

M.C. rubbed her frizzy yellow hair. "You girls . . . Why can't you get along?"

"Can I be excused?" Mads asked. "To practice my lines?"

M.C. nodded, but she looked pained. "Go ahead, honey."

I'll audition, if that's what she wants, Mads thought as she ran up to her room. *But she'll regret it. I'll stink up the place so badly M.C. will cringe with embarrassment. She'll think twice before trying to blackmail me again.*

3 News from Dan

To:	linaonme
From:	your daily horoscope

HERE IS TODAY'S HOROSCOPE: CANCER: An era is ending. It's put up or shut up time. I recommend shutting up, but if you decide to put up, good luck.

Larissa—

I haven't heard from you in a while. How is India? Long flight I guess, right? I'd love to hear your impressions of it. You used to describe San Francisco so beautifully, I'm sure you could make Mumbai come alive for someone who's never been there.

There is at last a little news in my humdrum suburban life— I've been offered a job at a private school in Portland

(Oregon, not Maine). Teaching English, which, as you
know, I've wanted to do for a long time. No more
Interpersonal Human Development! Can't say that I'll
miss it. Although I will miss a few things about good old
Rosewood, and a few of the people, too. . . .
Anyway, I'm pretty sure I'm going to accept the job. I'm off to
Portland this summer! It's not India, but I'm looking
forward to a change. I hope the Bollywood Film School
is treating you well. Write back soon.
—Beau

I don't believe it, Lina thought. *Ramona was right. The rumor
is true!*

Dan is leaving RSAGE. Leaving town! Forever!

A couple of months earlier, Lina had found a personal
ad online. The screen name was "Beauregard" but the
photo showed Dan Shulman, Lina's Interpersonal Human
Development teacher and the love of her life. Lina wrote
to "Beau" using the name "Larissa." Knowing that Dan
would never be interested in a romantic correspondence
with one of his students, she pretended to be a 22-year-
old graduate student. And it was fun for a while. Beau fell
for Larissa a little bit and wanted to meet her. That's when
the trouble began.

Lina had set up a lunch date and had gone to the

restaurant. But in the end, she couldn't go through with it. So she wrote to him explaining that she couldn't see him because she was moving to India. It nearly broke her heart to do it. But she had no choice. If Dan knew she was Larissa, he'd stop writing to her. The whole thing would be ruined.

But now he was moving away. After the end of the year, she'd never see him again. Things were ruined anyway.

Mads and Holly knew that Lina had a crush on Dan, but Lina's real feelings, the true depth of them, were more private. Lina was afraid her friends wouldn't understand. The one person who knew best how Lina felt—and even she didn't quite get it—was Ramona Fernandez, over-the-top Goth girl extraordinaire. Ramona's crush on Dan was almost as big as Lina's, and she showed it by wearing a skinny tie like Dan's around her neck every day, on top of her gauzy Goth clothes. Some of her friends wore the ties too. Ramona called it the Dan Shulman Cult. They even had a shrine to him in Ramona's room. Lina wasn't crazy about the ties and the cult but she put up with Ramona because she understood what Dan-love was all about.

Lina IMed Ramona immediately.

linaonme: huge news! U were right! He's leaving!

Lina knew that she didn't have to tell Ramona who "he" was. Their impossible love for Dan was just about the only thing Lina and Ramona had in common.

raven7: how do u know?

linaonme: he wrote me. as beauregard. He's moving to portland for a new job!

raven7: this is a nightmare! What r we going to do?

linaonme: I don't know. But we have to do something before
he leaves—or we'll regret it for the rest of our lives.

4 The Rabbit-Faced Boy of Her Dreams

To:	hollygolitely
From:	your daily horoscope

HERE IS TODAY'S HOROSCOPE: CAPRICORN: You can try to play God, but He'll always be more authentic in the role.

J osh is meeting us at the party," Rob said.

"Good," Holly said. "Is he wearing something nice?"

Rob stared at Holly. "How should I know?"

Boys. Holly let it go. It didn't really matter anyway. Boys all dressed pretty much alike. Holly stopped at the door of the Fowlers' house and gave Rob a quick kiss. "Thanks for helping me set this up."

Holly had searched and searched for the right boy

for Britta, and finally settled on a friend of Rob's named Josh Sisson. He was a senior, going to Berkeley in the fall, so he had to be pretty smart. Other than that, his main qualification was that his girlfriend had just dumped him. He was upset about it, needed cheering up, and wanted a new girlfriend to parade around in front of the old one as quickly as possible. When Holly heard that Nick Henin, a senior, was having a big party, she decided it was the perfect chance to lure Britta out of her self-imposed convent.

"I'm not sure this is going to work out," Rob said as Holly pressed the doorbell. "I mean, what do they have in common?"

"Well, they both wear glasses," Holly said. Josh wore heavy, black-framed ironic-hipster glasses. "At least there's that." It would have to do. "Anything could happen," Holly added. "They could fall in love at first sight. The course of true love is uncontrollable and unpredictable."

"Who said that?" Rob asked.

"I did," Holly said. "But it sounds like a real quotation, doesn't it?"

Peggy Fowler answered the door. "Holly! Nice to see you, Rob." She let them in, fluttering nervously to the stairs. "Britta! Holly's here!" She turned back to Holly and Rob, waiting in the foyer. "Britta tells me you're introducing her to a boy tonight? I hope he's nice."

"Very nice, Mrs. Fowler," Holly said. "He's a friend of Rob's."

"Good. So he's not too wild or anything, right? I want Britta to have more of a social life but not so much that her studies suffer, know what I mean? Drugs and drinking can just *erase* your brain cells . . . "

"Josh isn't a big partier, Mrs. Fowler," Rob said. "Britta's brain cells will be safe with him."

Britta came down the stairs in a neat blue skirt, preppy white sweater and a headband holding back her curly hair. They left the house and climbed into Rob's mother's big black SUV. They drove a couple of miles to Nick Henin's house, where they were meeting Josh, Lina, Mads and Stephen.

Nick's house was a big, showy glass cube at the end of a quiet street. The Henins had gotten rich off a candy bar made especially for people allergic to peanuts. The cube glowed in the night, and through the windows Holly could already see a crush of mingling bodies.

Lina, Mads, and Stephen met them near the front door. Mads, small, dark-haired and creamy-skinned, was dressed for action in platform sandals and a mini-skirt. Stephen, tall and thin with straight brown hair and an air of sophistication about him—at least compared to the oafs around him—held her hand. Holly was glad to see things were going well with them. They'd only been dating a short time, but Mads had wanted a boyfriend for so long, and it looked like Stephen was going to be her first real one.

"It's packed," Lina shouted over the music. "I think every kid in town is here." Holly was surprised to see that she was wearing purple eye shadow and mascara on her brown almond-shaped eyes. Tallish, athletic, with shiny black hair, Lina wasn't usually a big makeup wearer, other than lip gloss.

"Hi, Britta," Mads said. "Are you nervous?"

Britta shot an annoyed glance at Holly. "Did you tell everyone that you're fixing me up tonight?"

"No," Holly said. "Just Mads and Lina. They're my Dating Game partners. We always consult each other on matches."

"There's Josh," Rob said, nodding toward a sandy-haired boy with heavy black glasses. He was sitting on the chrome-and-leather couch in the living room, spotted Rob, and waved. Mentally Holly gave him her stamp of approval. How could Britta go wrong? He was quick to smile and nicely balanced between cool and geeky. Britta's first love. *She should thank me,* Holly thought. Since they'd started the Dating Game, Holly had made many success-ful matches, and she was proud of her record.

Holly followed Rob to the couch, dragging Britta behind her. "That's him?" Britta whispered.

"Isn't he cute?" Holly said.

Britta didn't answer. Holly said hello to Josh and introduced Britta. "We'll go get some drinks," Holly said. "Rob, come with me?"

She and Rob walked to the open kitchen and peeked back at the happy couple. "Do you think he likes her?" Holly asked.

"They've only known each other two seconds," Rob said.

They grabbed some sodas and waited a few minutes before turning back to watch Josh and Britta. Josh sat down on the couch and gestured to Britta to sit next to him. Britta hesitated. She looked around the room. Then she shook her head, said something, and walked away.

"What is she doing?" Holly whispered. She dropped the drinks on a table and chased after Britta. Rob made a beeline for Josh.

Holly caught up with Britta as she was about to enter the bathroom. *All right,* Holly thought, *maybe everything is okay. She just had to go to the bathroom.*

"I'll be right out," Britta said. Holly waited. A few minutes later Britta reappeared.

"Can we go now?" Britta asked. "I'm ready to leave."

"What? Don't you want to talk to Josh for a few minutes?"

"No. I don't like him."

Holly couldn't believe it. "How can you not like him? You hardly know him."

"I just don't. I could tell as soon as I saw him that he wasn't right for me. Sorry."

Holly clenched her teeth to keep herself from snapping at Britta.

"Go back there and talk to him," Holly said. "You haven't given him a chance. You can't tell anything just by looking at him. And besides, what's wrong with the way he looks? I think he's cute."

"I just don't like him, that's all," Britta said. "So can we leave?"

"We just got here," Holly said. "Give it a little more time. Even if you don't hit it off with Josh, you might have fun. Talk to people! Relax!"

"Okay," Britta said. "I'll try."

"I'm going over to talk to Rob and Josh," Holly said. "Want to come with me?"

"I think I'll take a look around the house," Britta said.

Rob was sitting with Josh. "What's going on?" Josh asked when Holly sat next to him.

Holly shrugged. "I'm sorry, Josh. What can I tell you?

She's not used to parties. I think she's just nervous."

"Nervous?" Rob said. "She spent two seconds with Josh before she ran away. That goes beyond nervous. That's more into crazy territory."

"All right, *extremely* nervous," Holly said. "I left her sulking outside the bathroom."

"So . . . she doesn't like me?" Josh asked. He looked hurt, and Holly felt terrible.

"Yeah, Holly," Rob demanded. "What's her problem?"

"It's not that," Holly lied. "She's never had a boyfriend before, and I guess she's still not ready. Don't worry, Josh. You won't have any trouble finding a new girlfriend."

"Seems to me I'm already having trouble," Josh said.

"It's not you, it's her," Holly said. "And I'm not just saying that."

Holly and Rob spent another hour reassuring Josh that he wasn't the biggest loser at the party. They finally got him to go outside with them and sit on the deck where Mads, Stephen, and Lina were sipping beer. Holly was annoyed with Britta—how could she be so snotty?—and avoided her until the party started winding down, when she finally wondered where Britta was and what she'd been doing all this time.

She found Britta sitting on the spiral staircase, deep in an intense conversation with a guy. He had short black hair and an unremarkable face except for a slight overbite that made Holly think of a rabbit. He was dressed kind of farmerishly in a red flannel shirt and dark jeans. Holly had never seen him before.

"Britta," Holly said. "Are you ready to go home now?"

Britta turned, her eyes shining, her face calm and happy as if she'd been hypnotized.

"Already?" she said. "It's still early."

"No, it isn't," Holly said. "It's almost midnight."

"Oh. I guess I'd better go," Britta said to the guy.

"Wait," he said, taking a pen and a scrap of paper from his pocket. He handed them to Britta, and she scribbled something down.

"Who was that guy?" Holly asked Britta at the door.

"His name is Ed Reyes," Britta said in a gushy, awestruck voice. "And he's the most wonderful guy who ever walked the earth."

"What?" Holly glanced back at the guy, who waved to Britta. "He looks pretty average to me." *Possibly even below average*, she thought, but she kept this to herself.

"He's amazing," Britta said. "Holly, I think I'm in love."

5 Touched

HERE IS TODAY'S HOROSCOPE: VIRGO: When you play with guns, there's always a chance you'll shoot yourself in the foot.

O h, Papa, I know what you're thinking. I can read minds now, remember?" Mads stood spotlit on stage at the Carlton Bay Playhouse, eyes closed, rubbing her temples in her best—or rather, worst—imitation of a girl reading someone's mind. She was doing a scene from *Touched*. In the front row sat M.C., Audrey, and the director, Charles Huang, and a few other people associated with the theater. Backstage, other auditioning actors watched as Mads chewed the scenery.

"You're wondering why the cows won't give up any milk," Mads said. "You're wondering if you're going to lose your dairy farm. But Papa, if you'd only listen to me! I know why the cows have gone dry. It's the Visitors, Papa. They scared the cows. The Visitors from the Great Behind!"

Her eyes popped open dramatically and she threw her arm into the air as if pointing meaningfully toward the sky. The actors backstage tittered. M.C. called from her seat, *"Beyond*, honey. The line is `Visitors from the Great Beyond.'"

"Oh, sorry," Mads said, even though she'd done it on purpose. It was her third mistake so far. The audition was going even worse than she'd planned. "Should I try it again?"

"That won't be necessary," Charles Huang said. "Just finish the scene and you'll be done."

Finally. Mads spat out the last few lines. "Did you ever hear of ESP, Papa? Because I think I have it. I think I have Extra-Sensory Perspiration."

More giggling from backstage. Mads took a bow. "Thank you, Madison," Charles said, not bothering to correct her. "Nice job. Next—"

Mads left the stage and sat beside her mother. "You stank," Audrey whispered. "I told you she would suck."

"Honey, what happened up there?" M.C. asked. "I've never heard you make so many mistakes before."

Mads shrugged. "Stage fright, I guess." *They'd have to be insane to cast me now,* she thought with satisfaction. *I don't have to do the play, and I still get to go to Stanford with Holly! My life is golden!*

"Anyway, I'm out of here," Mads said, gathering up her bag. She'd brought her bike to the theater, knowing that M.C. would be there all afternoon watching boring auditions. Mads had done her part; she didn't want to hang around any longer.

"Be careful on the roads, honey," M.C. said. "Do you want to go with her, Audrey, or stay?"

"Stay," Audrey said with grim determination. She wanted to see every actress auditioning for Little Mariah. Audrey wanted that part, and she needed to reassure herself that the competition wasn't good enough to override her obvious advantage of being the playwright's daughter.

"Fine, bore yourself to death," Mads said. She started up the aisle. The theater door opened, casting a shaft of blinding sunlight into the darkened auditorium. Mads reached for the door, passing the two people who'd just come in. She looked back at them. It was Jane Cotham— and Sean! What were they doing there?

"Hey, kid," Sean said as he followed Jane down the aisle.

The sight of him—especially so suddenly, so

unexpectedly—jolted Mads. She stopped and watched them, dazed, until they disappeared backstage. Sean. He was like a force field to her. And Stephen wasn't there to counteract his power.

Should she go back in? Should she stay and find out what he was doing there?

Thank god he didn't see my audition! Mads thought. *But maybe someone will tell him about it—like Audrey. I'd better get out of here.*

She unlocked her bike and pedaled home, wondering at every block if she should turn and go back. There was only one obvious reason why Sean would be at the theater: he was auditioning for a part in the play! And Teen Mariah had a boyfriend—and she got to kiss him. What if Sean got that part?

Mads wanted to kick herself. *I should never have blown my audition!* she thought. *What if I've missed a chance to kiss Sean?*

6 True Love Defined

To:	hollygolitely
From:	your daily horoscope

HERE IS TODAY'S HOROSCOPE: CAPRICORN: You're getting mushy on me, Capricorn. Bring back your old hardheaded self—please!

I can't believe how different you look," Holly said to Britta at lunch on Monday. Instead of her usual nondescript overalls or baggy corduroys, Britta was wearing a pretty burgundy skirt and a clingy white knit top. She hadn't cut her hair or changed her glasses, but her face glowed. She was blooming.

"Thank you," she said. "I feel different, too. Holly, you were right. There's so much more to life than studying!"

They settled in a corner of the lunchroom by the window. It was the last lunch period of the day and the room was clearing out.

What could have brought about such a sudden change in Britta? Holly was dying to know. "Tell me everything," she said.

"I can't believe it's only been three days since I met him!" Britta said, speaking of Ed Reyes, the boy she met at Nick Henin's party. "It feels like a lifetime."

Aha! Holly's matchmaking prowess strikes again! Okay, so Ed wasn't the match she had planned for Britta. The important thing was that she saw a void in Britta's life and helped her fill it.

"He picked me up at noon on Saturday and we spent the whole day together," Britta said. "I mean the *whole* day. I didn't get home until after midnight! I've never done anything like that before. My parents didn't know what to think."

Holly tried to remember if she and Rob had ever done that. "What did you do all day?"

"For a while we just drove around and talked. He told me all about himself, and I told him all about myself. Not that there's much to tell. But he's so interesting. He's a sophomore in college in England! But his father lives here. So he's visiting. We drove to the beach and we found this adorable little house, with nothing else around it, right on the water, with a 'For Sale' sign out front. And Ed said, 'Let's look inside.' I was afraid to. I mean, it's trespassing, and anyway I thought the door would probably be locked. But it wasn't. So we went inside. It's the sweetest little house! It's completely empty and the electricity is turned off and everything. But you can see the ocean from the second floor, and hear the waves . . . "

Holly imagined Ed and Britta holding hands like a newlywed couple, pushing open the door of a pretty little vine-covered house filled with a watery light from the sea. "It sounds so romantic," Holly said.

"We sat on the floor and talked some more. He's really smart. But he's had a hard time with his parents and every-thing . . . Then we got hungry, so we got back in the car. We couldn't find a place to eat that seemed right. We were in this particular mood, you know, and we didn't want to ruin it by going to some noisy restaurant. So Ed pulled into a shopping center and told me to wait in the car. A few minutes later he came out with two big shopping bags and drove off. I asked him where we were going and he said it was a surprise."

Holly raised an eyebrow. After all, Britta barely knew this guy. "Were you scared?"

"Scared?" Britta said. "Why?"

Holly shrugged. "I mean it was nighttime and he wouldn't tell you where he was taking you—"

"You wouldn't say that if you knew him," Britta said. "He took me back to the house. The little house by the ocean. He'd bought a flashlight and candles and a blanket and some takeout food and everything. We sneaked inside and he lit some candles and we had a romantic dinner right there on the floor of the house."

Holly was impressed. "Oh my god! That is incredible."

"I know," Britta said. "We stepped out on the deck and looked at the moon on the water. And he kissed me."

"Wow." Holly closed her eyes. Why didn't anything like this ever happen to her? Holly wondered. It was like a dream!

"My parents wanted to kill me by the time I got home. He wanted to see me again last night but I was afraid they'd say no. I mean, Sunday night. A school night. So I told them I was going to meet you at Vineland to study." Vineland was a popular café.

Holly's eyes popped open. "You did?"

"And I sneaked back to the little house to meet him. But on the way I stopped to pick up some food and we had another romantic dinner."

Holly wanted to go back a step and clarify something. "You told your parents you were with me?"

"You don't mind, do you?"

"Well, no, but you should have asked me first. I didn't go out last night. What if your mother talks to Jen and finds out?"

"You're right. . . . Next time I'll warn you."

"Okay."

"It's just that he's here for such a short time—only a few weeks!" Britta said. "So we have to spend every possible minute together."

They were really in love. Holly was blown away. She didn't know anybody who was this much in love. Not where the love was mutual, anyway. Sure, Mads loved Sean but he hardly knew she was alive. And Lina and Dan . . . that wasn't even worth thinking about. Holly didn't think of Mads' and Lina's crushes as real love. They were impossible, unattainable. Nothing would ever come of them, either one. But this . . . this was different.

It had all happened so fast—and to Britta of all people.

Holly thought about the last evening she spent with Rob. Saturday night, she went over to his house. They played video games. Holly actually liked video games; some of them, anyway. And she remembered thinking what a good time she had with Rob. They didn't have to do anything special; they got along so well they could just pal around like buddies.

Like buddies. While Britta and Ed were having candlelight dinners in an abandoned beach house, she and Rob were blasting aliens and making nachos in the microwave. It was like two different worlds. One so immature and everyday—so high school—and the other so passionate and romantic. Worldly. Grown-up. Serious. Holly envied Britta. Suddenly her own life seemed humdrum, drab, excitement-free. Pathetic.

"It's incredible," Holly said to Lina and Mads at Vineland later that afternoon. "I mean, did you see her today? She's transformed."

"It's true, I almost didn't recognize her," Lina said. "She looked lighter, or something."

"And she suddenly has a fashion sense," Mads said. "How did that happen?"

"It's—it's true love," Holly said. "I think it is."

"They only met three days ago," Lina said.

"She hardly knows him," Mads added. "How could it be true love already?"

"It was love at first sight," Holly insisted. "Mads, you of all people—"

"Say no more." Mads held her hand out to stop Holly from going further. "I know what you are going to say, Boobmeister, and you're wrong. Sure, I fell in love with

Sean at first sight, but I never said it was *true* love."

"For one thing, Sean doesn't love her back," Lina said.

"Well, and for another thing—" Mads didn't want to dwell on that aspect of it "—I'm with Stephen now, so how can it be true love if we're both with other people? Plus I really like Stephen and I might fall in love with him, too, who knows?"

"What about you, Lina?" Holly said. "You won't even date anyone, you're so crazy about Dan."

"That's not true," Lina said. "I just haven't found the right guy yet. And anyway, Dan is a perfect example. My love for him may be true, but it can't last, because he's leaving."

"Oh, yeah, I heard that," Mads said. "What life form are they going to dig up to teach IHD next year?"

"Luckily we won't be sophomores anymore and it won't matter to us by then," Holly said. Needless to say, Holly and Mads had nowhere near the same feelings for Dan that Lina did.

"Thanks for the sympathy," Lina said.

"I feel bad for you, I really do," Mads said.

"It's just that we think it will be good for you to finally forget about him," Holly said. "And move on with your life."

"Yeah, like join us here in the real world," Mads said.

"So much happens in high school," Lina said. "People moving and changing. . . . It's rough on love. Especially true love."

"Define true love," Holly said.

"Soul mates," Lina said. "A meeting of the minds."

"The perfect match," Mads added. "Stars in alignment, all systems go."

"Ed and Britta could have that," Holly said.

"They could," Mads said. "But you don't know for sure yet."

"Too early to tell," Lina said.

"If you talked to her, you'd know," Holly said.

"True love has to be proven," Lina said. "Maybe love can strike you in a second, but only time will tell if the love is really true."

"There are too many fakeouts," Mads said. "You can't just assume. Look at Autumn and that guy Trent. She thought it was true love and it lasted a week tops." Autumn was notoriously high-maintenance.

"Yeah, but look at Autumn and Vince," Holly said. "They've lasted two whole months!" Holly had matched Autumn with Vince Overbeck herself. Everyone said Autumn would eat him alive, but instead they fell into a sloppy, drooly, disgustingly public love. Chalk up another success for Holly, though, to be honest, she sort of regretted setting up that match.

"That can't be true love," Mads said. "Autumn doesn't have it in her. And it's too gross."

"Mads is right," Lina said. "Autumn doesn't have the soul. Anyway, high school puts a lot of wear and tear on a relationship. Sure, maybe it can last a month. But can it last all the way to graduation, and beyond? It has to be very special."

"There are so many temptations in high school," Mads said. "Other guys. Hormones. Interfering friends. Mood swings. Look how much Britta changed in one weekend! Suppose she'd already had a boyfriend before. He'd be history now."

"Yeah, but she *didn't* have a boyfriend before," Holly said. "That's the whole point."

"Exactly," Mads said.

"What?" Holly said.

"I'm getting confused," Lina said.

"Stop ganging up on me, you guys," Holly said. "Let's see what everybody else at school thinks. Can true love survive high school? And what is true love anyway?"

QUIZ: IS IT TRUE LOVE?

It was love at first sight—or was it?

How can you tell the real thing from a fleeting attraction?

1. **When you think of him, you think of:**
   a ▶ his face
   b ▶ his voice
   c ▶ his body
   d ▶ the fact that he still owes you five dollars for pizza from the other night

2. **To you he smells like:**
   a ▶ fresh bread
   b ▶ soap
   c ▶ wet dog
   d ▶ sauerkraut (and you don't like sauerkraut)

3. **When you see him you hear:**
   a ▶ a heavenly choir
   b ▶ violins
   c ▶ a talk radio station
   d ▶ fingernails on a chalkboard

4. **On your first date he gave you:**
   a ▶ a love poem

b ▶ flowers

c ▶ nothing

d ▶ the flu

5. Your first words to him were:

    a ▶ "I think I'm in love."

    b ▶ "Nice shirt."

    c ▶ "Is this the line for the bathroom?"

    d ▶ "Move it, Tubby!"

6. He's like his father because:

    a ▶ he's honest

    b ▶ he works hard

    c ▶ he snores

    d ▶ he has a pot belly

7. Your favorite thing about him is:

    a ▶ the way he respects you

    b ▶ the way he listens to you

    c ▶ the way you look together

    d ▶ the way he fades into the woodwork when you don't need
    him

8. Your favorite time with him is:

    a ▶ alone together, kissing

b ▶ on the phone, talking late at night

c ▶ those funny little silences that prove you don't have to talk to be close

d ▶ watching him drive away

9. If you had to describe him in one phrase, you'd call him:

a ▶ king of men

b ▶ nice

c ▶ adequate

d ▶ scum

Scoring:

If you chose mostly a's, you've found bliss. True love! Just keep an eye on it so it won't go sour.

If you chose mostly b's, you have a perfectly good relationship. Maybe it will blossom into true love later—you never know.

If you chose mostly c's, you're biding your time with someone who doesn't really grab you. Let go and find someone who makes your heart race.

If you chose mostly d's, nuff said. You're either cynically using your honey or else you think this is how love should be. Don't settle! And get out of this trap before you turn bitter!

"Even if we settle on the definition of true love, that doesn't answer the question," Lina said. "Which is: Can true love survive the pressures and changes of high school?"

"I think it could," Holly said.

"Maybe," Mads said.

A Dating Game Poll: Can True Love Survive High School? What Is True Love Anyway? Tell us your opinion.

smartee: True love is when you meet the one person in the whole world who's meant for you. And what are the chances of that? They must be a zillion to one! So forget about high school, true love hardly exists anywhere.

dandylyon: High school boys aren't capable of true love. They're too selfish. There, I said it.

grit55: What about girls? All they care about is who's popular and what presents you buy them. They're too shallow for true love.

paco: Can true love be one-way? Because I love a girl and she doesn't love me back. But still, on my end, it feels like true love. She just doesn't know it yet.

smartee: No, true love definitely has to be two-way. That's why it's so rare.

martianboy: My mother says my dad is her true love, and they fight all the time. Plus he burps at the dinner table. If that's true love, who needs it?

bubba27: True love is a football game on the tube, a hot
pizza, a liter of Coke and my mom's fudge brownies—
end of story. And yes, it will last the rest of my life,
thank you very much.

"You watch," Mads said. "Britta and Ed will be in love till he has to leave, and then they'll e-mail for a while, and then she'll meet another guy, and that will be that. The whole thing will last two months."

"We'll see," Holly said. "I still say this is the real thing."

7 Close Encounter

To:	linaonme
From:	your daily horoscope

HERE IS TODAY'S HOROSCOPE: CANCER: You're totally clueless today. What's the problem? Tired? Iron-poor blood? Wax in your ears?

Varsity Lax Squad Foiled by Streaker
by Lina Ozu

A streaker brought chaos to the boys' varsity lacrosse game against Draper High today, distracting forward Barton Mitchell and possibly causing him to miss a shot to the goal and lose the game for the Rosewood Thorns. The tubby streaker, later identified as a Draper junior, was accused of purposely trying to distract the Thorns at a crucial moment in the game. The score was tied 2-2 when the Thorns advanced on Draper's goal . . .

"Hey, Lina." Lina stopped typing and looked up from the sports article she was writing. The office of the *Seer*, Rosewood's school newspaper, was quiet and empty in the late afternoon. Or it had been, until Walker Moore came in. Lina was glad for the company.

"Hey, Walker. Did you cover the swim meet this afternoon?" Lina asked.

"Yeah. We lost," Walker said. "I hate writing up the losses."

"Me, too," Lina said.

"How did the lax team do?"

"Lost," Lina said. "But I got a good story out of it."

Walker stood behind her and read what she'd typed on the computer monitor. He laughed.

"I heard about that streaker guy," Walker said. "You get all the good stories. Did anyone get a photo of him?"

"I got one, from the back," Lina said. "But Kate vetoed it. No nudity in the school paper." Kate Bryson was the *Seer*'s editor-in-chief.

"Another Ozu classic. Right place, right time— you've got the knack." Walker sat down at a computer terminal and started typing. He was long-legged and thin with a loose-limbed, relaxed way about him. Lina knew he was handsome, with pale brown skin, green eyes, and short, spiky hair. The problem was she didn't really care. Nobody looked really handsome to her except for Dan.

"I've got to change the spelling of a name in one of my stories," Walker said. "Did you know Jim Krcic spells his name K-R-C—"

Lina tuned out. She liked Walker but she had other things on her mind just then. Like finishing this lacrosse article before five, when she had to meet Ramona at the marina to make plans. Extra-important Dan plans. They had to find a way to get to him before he moved away, and time was running out.

"Anyway, I'm having a few friends over to my house tonight if you feel like dropping by," Walker was saying when she finally logged off and started gathering up her things. "Nothing big, just a casual hang. We might watch a movie or something."

"That sounds like fun," Lina said, without being completely sure what he was talking about. It was almost five; she was going to be late. The marina was a good fifteen-minute bike ride from school. Not that she cared about keeping Ramona waiting, but sometimes Ramona lashed out about things like that, and Lina just didn't want to hear about it.

Lina started for the door. "So I'll see you later?" Walker said.

"Yep. See you later," Lina said. "Bye."

She hurried outside, jumped on her bike, and pedaled toward the water. Carlton Bay was full of boat piers and seafood restaurants and a weathered boardwalk that ran along the Marina.

Ramona was waiting for her on a bench—her own bike leaning against a rail—licking an ice-cream cone. The pink ice cream clashed with her raven hair, ragged black dress and tights, green nails, and elaborate mask of Goth makeup. Around her neck she wore a thin orange tie, a symbol of her love for Dan, who always wore skinny ties. Lina was used to Ramona's style by now, but it had taken a while.

"Sit down, we've got to talk fast," Ramona said. "I don't have that much time. My mom's having trouble unloading a house and she wants me to do my voodoo thing on the buyers."

Ramona was into spells and love potions and stuff. Her mother was a real estate agent and seemed down-to-earth, but it looked as if Ramona was drawing her into her web. Lina would have thought real estate was immune to the forces of the supernatural, but obviously she was wrong.

"First of all," Ramona said, "I surrender him to you."

"What?" Ramona was nearly as in love with Dan as Lina was, and very competitive. It wasn't like her to surrender anything to anyone.

"Look, there's no time to fool around," Ramona said. "Only one of us can have him, right? I mean, if you look at it realistically. And that's what we've got to do—be realistic. So, you're the one who's been secretly e-mailing him and all. Once we get him, he's yours. I just want to live vicariously through you. But you have to promise to tell me every detail, no matter how personal or gross. Promise?"

"I promise."

"Really? Do you swear? Do I have to extract some kind of elaborate vow from you?"

"No, you can trust me, Ramona. You know that."

"I do *not* know that, but I don't have much choice. Now. How are we going to get him?"

Lina thought a minute. "Um, what are we talking about, exactly? What do you mean, 'get him'?"

"Well, you know . . . " Ramona trailed off. That was the thing about loving a teacher. You longed, you yearned, but for what exactly? It was so unlikely you'd get anywhere with him that you didn't have to think that far ahead.

"You're going to be his girlfriend," Ramona finally announced.

And that was what Lina wanted. But somehow she found it hard to picture.

"We'll start slow," Ramona said. "What we want, by, say, the end of the month, is for him to think of you as different from the other students. Special."

Secretly, Lina hoped he already felt this way. "That's not enough."

"Okay. The two of you have to be somewhere alone together. Not school-related. And it has to be understood that what you're doing is not a student-teacher thing, but a guy-girl thing."

"It's kind of vague—"

"I've got it. We'll send him a note from 'a secret admirer' and get him to meet us somewhere. You'll go up to him with a black veil over your face, so he can't see who you are, and then—"

"Ramona—" Lina elbowed her in the ribs. A familiar figure was walking toward them down the boardwalk.

"What? I'm on a roll here. Then, when the moment is right, you rip off the veil—"

"Ramona! Look!" Lina nodded at the man, who was coming closer. It was him. Dan.

Ramona clutched Lina's arm. "Oh my god! It's him!

I conjured him with my psychic brain waves! I knew I had powers!"

"Ow—Ramona, your claws are digging into my skin." Lina peeled Ramona's hand off her arm.

"This is a sign," Ramona whispered. "This is our moment. We've got to act NOW!"

"How? What are we going to do?"

"Just go!" Ramona yanked Lina to her feet. Dan had nearly reached them.

"Ramona, stop it!" Lina whispered. "I thought you had to go home and cast a spell on some real estate."

"That can wait."

"At least tell me what the plan is!"

Ramona said nothing. She pushed Lina into Dan's path. He couldn't help but notice her—she was blocking his way.

"Hi, girls," he said mildly.

Lina stared at his thin frame, clad as usual in a vintage suit. That day he wore a particularly cool skinny tie, gray-green with a single horizontal red stripe across the middle. It was amazing that after all she'd been through with him—the pseudonymous e-mails, the aborted secret lunch in the city, months of sitting in class listening to him stammer out educational information about sex and relationships, even the occasional private student-teacher conference—in spite of all that, she still melted at the sight of him, still got tongue-tied. At that moment, her tongue felt as if it had swollen to the size of a Mallomar. It filled her mouth uncomfortably and refused to move.

"Hi, Dan," Ramona said. RSAGE was the kind of school where you could call your teachers by their first names. "It's disgustingly sunny out, isn't it? I wish it would rain again. Where are you off to?"

"The Marina Café," Dan said. "What are you two doing?"

Lina had stepped out of his direct path, so he started walking again, slowly. Ramona and Lina walked along with him.

"Just sitting on a bench discussing what a downer life is," Ramona said.

"Come on, Ramona," Dan said. "Is life really so bad?"

"If you look at it straight, without all the filters our society imposes on it—yes," Ramona said. "Life sucks. But I don't have to tell *you* that. You're a man of the world, intelligent and all. You know the score."

Lina watched Dan's face. His pale eyebrows twitched slightly. He was trying not to roll his eyes at Ramona's ridiculousness. Lina was sure of it.

"Anyway, until we're ready to slough off our mortal coils, we still have to eat," Ramona said. "We were just saying we wanted to stop somewhere for a snack. Weren't we, Lina?"

Lina nodded. "Um, yes." They were getting closer to the Marina Café. Lina could see that most of the outside tables were full. A group of six or so was just settling down at a large round table on the deck.

"Well, there are plenty of good places to eat around here," Dan said.

"But the Marina Café is one of my favorites," Ramona said. "Always has been. It's a little pricey, but worth it."

They had almost reached the café. Something about that group of six was starting to look familiar. That tall, balding guy in the brown suit, for example—he looked an awful lot like John Alvarado, the principal of RSAGE. And that round lady with curly gray hair . . . Was that—? It was. Mildred Weymouth, the geometry teacher. Known to the students as Mildew.

"Well," Ramona was saying, "since we're all hungry and we're all headed in the same direction, why don't we all eat together?"

No! Lina elbowed Ramona. Didn't she see? Dan was going to some kind of teacher get-together—and Ramona was trying to get them invited.

"Well, I guess you can join me, if you really want to," Dan said.

"Great!" Ramona said.

They had reached the café. Camille Barker, the pretty young French teacher, sat beside Alvarado, with Frank Welling, the art teacher, on her other side. Lina wanted to grab Ramona's head and force her to look at where they were going. Dan stopped, and Ramona finally tore her eyes away from him and saw the table full of teachers. She stopped dead in her tracks.

"I'm sure we can fit you girls in somewhere," Dan said.

"Thanks, Dan, but we were in more of a milkshake mood," Lina said. Finally her tongue loosened up. "Right, Ramona?"

"Yes, milkshake, definitely." Ramona started to back away from the café as if it were a hangout for the undead. Actually, the undead would probably have appealed to her. Nothing was worse than off-duty teachers. Dan excepted, of course.

"Really? Too bad," Dan said. "Well, see you girls at school." He walked through the opening in the gate that separated the café's deck from the boardwalk, waving to his colleagues. Ramona grabbed Lina and they ran back toward the bench they had come from.

"Look what you almost got us into!" Lina said. "You're too impulsive. You shouldn't have pushed me in front of him without a plan."

"Well, you could have said something and helped me out. You didn't open your mouth the whole time. You made me do all the work."

"We can't just throw ourselves at him," Lina said. "We have to think carefully about what we're doing."

"You're right," Ramona said. "This is a delicate operation. Tonight, before you go to sleep, pray to the Goddess of Girlpower to send you a brilliant idea. Say, 'Oh mighty Isis, infuse me with your wisdom of love—'"

"I'm not doing that," Lina said.

"I'll do it, then," Ramona said. "You always make me do everything."

"Walker!" Lina called. She spotted him between classes the next afternoon, weaving through the hall toward her locker. She'd been looking for him all day. "I've got to ask you something. You had Modern World History last year, right? What did you do for your final project?"

"What?" Walker looked surprised at her question. "Let me ask *you* something. What happened to you last night?"

"Last night?" Lina didn't know what he was talking about. Did he mean why did she spend an hour before bed praying to Isis to send her a brilliant Dan plan? Probably not. How would he know about that?

"Remember? I had people over?"

Oh, yeah. She vaguely remembered him mentioning something about that in the newspaper office. After the run-in with Dan she completely forgot about it. But she never said she'd go—did she?

"Walker, I'm sorry I missed your get-together," Lina said. "I didn't think it was a big deal."

"It wasn't a big deal." He seemed hurt. She couldn't understand why. Did the whole party hinge on her being there? "But you said you'd come. I was expecting you, that's all."

"I didn't say I'd come," Lina said.

"Yes, you did," Walker said. "You said, 'I'll see you later.'"

Lina struggled to remember her exact words upon leaving the newsroom. Her mind hadn't been on Walker. She'd hardly heard anything he'd said. How could she remember her exact words, especially when they were so mundane? But she thought she could see where the mix-up was. "I didn't mean literally 'I will see you later.' I just meant, you know, 'See you. Later.' As in, good-bye?"

"Oh." Walker shifted his books from his hip to his chest. "I guess I misunderstood. Sorry. I thought you'd somehow turned into the kind of person who doesn't keep her word. But I was wrong. Good to know."

He walked away. Lina shook her head. What was *that* all about?

8 A Lady of the Theater

| To: | mad4u |
| From: | your daily horoscope |

HERE IS TODAY'S HOROSCOPE: VIRGO: First you're in, then you're out . . . quit flip-flopping and make up your mind.

Mama, you've come back! Oh, Mama, I'm so glad you've come home safe and sound!"

Audrey flung herself at M.C. as she came in from the supermarket, loaded up with shopping bags. Mads was beginning to miss the old Pop-Tart version of her sister. At least she talked like a real human then.

M.C. struggled to the kitchen with Audrey wrapped around her. "You can let go, Audrey," she said. "But guess what? The Method must really work, because you got the part, Little Mariah."

"What?" Mads cried.

"What?!?" Audrey squealed. "I got the part! I did it! I did it! I got the part!" She hopped up and down, her braids bouncing. "I'm a real actress!"

"Big shock," Mads said. "Your mother is the play-wright. You kind of had an in."

"Charles promised me he wouldn't play favorites, Mads," M.C. said. "He swore he chose the best actors for each part."

"What about me?" Mads asked. "Am I doomed to walk the stage as Teen Mariah?"

"They'd be mental to cast *you*," Audrey said.

"Audrey, that's not nice." M.C. looked uncomfortable. "He hasn't cast that part yet, Mads. But . . . well, I wouldn't get your hopes up."

Mads wasn't surprised. She *had* really screwed up her audition. M.C. pulled a piece of paper from her bag and set it on the kitchen table. Then she started putting the groceries away.

Mads snatched up the paper. It was the unfinished cast list. Sure enough, next to "Little Mariah" was written "Audrey Markowitz." "Teen Mariah" was left blank. Mads scanned the list for Sean's name. No sign of it. She found the role of Buck, the boy who kisses Teen Mariah. That part was filled not by Sean but by someone named Damien Chopra. Whoever that was. But across from "Grown Mariah," which was Mariah as a young woman, was a name Mads did recognize: Jane Cotham.

Wow. Sean's girlfriend was going to be in the play. As Mads' mother.

Mads had heard about the kind of camaraderie that cropped up among actors on movie sets and in theater groups. That was what M.C. was hoping would develop between Mads and Audrey. Anyone in the play with Jane would probably get to know her pretty well. They'd spend hours together, sharing confidences, even secrets. They would talk about their boyfriends. . . . Think of all the things she could learn about Sean, if only she was in the play with Jane.

Suddenly, Mads wanted to be in the play more than she'd ever wanted anything.

Why did she have to screw up her audition so badly?

At least her part wasn't cast yet. "Mom?" she said. "I've been thinking . . . I didn't prepare very well for my audition. Do you think Charles would give me another chance, if I promise to work very hard?"

M.C. smiled at her. "Oh, Madison, I'm so proud of you!"

Mads went upstairs to e-mail Stephen. He was very interested in her career, or non-career, in the arts.

To: steverino

From: mad4u

Re: back in the saddle

guess what? I'm going to audition for teen mariah again. I
realize I was being immature about it before. This time I
won't mess up on purpose, only by accident. Like you
said, it could be a good experience for me. I've turned a
corner. I've grown. Aren't you proud of me?

What's nu w/u?

To: mad4u

From: steverino

Re: Re: back in the saddle

U r so mature now. you'll be a thespian! A lady of the theatuh.
I hope you'll let me walk down the red carpet with you
at the oscars.

Not much new here. studying. chem test tomorrow. Want to
try for lunch? r u free 5th period?

To: steverino

From: mad4u

Re: lunch

Yes, but only if you'll spend half the lunch period helping me
with my lines. Deal?

To: mad4u
From: steverino
Re: Re: lunch
Deal. Dad is making bbq chicken tonight—I'll bring you a leg.
xxx

"Thanks for coming with me, Lina," Mads said. They huddled backstage, waiting for Charles to call Mads for her second audition. "After the last time, I really need the support. God knows Audrey's no help."

"Try not to embarrass me, Fatison," Audrey sneered, using one of her favorite nicknames for Mads.

"I've been embarrassed since the day you were born," Mads shot back.

"I think you'll be okay this time," Lina said. She had helped Mads practice her lines. Holly had planned on coming to support Mads, too, but at the last minute she got a frantic phone call from Britta. Apparently, Britta was having some kind of love crisis. Holly didn't say what it was. But Mads wished Holly could be with her. Holly had a natural confidence that sometimes rubbed off on Mads. Mads hoped so, anyway.

"Madison? Are you ready?" Charles called.

Mads gripped Lina's hand. "Remember—it's the great *beyond*," Lina said, pushing her toward the stage.

Mads went out and performed a new monologue. This time she got every line right, no mistakes. She may have underacted a little, as an antidote to Audrey's hamminess. But she didn't stink. Not a bit.

When it was over, Charles, M.C., and Lina clapped loudly. "Very nice, Madison," Charles said. "Big improvement. Well, we're down to the wire with this role, since rehearsals begin this weekend, so I think I can safely say you have the part."

"All right!" Mads jumped up. Her plan was working perfectly. She was one step closer to learning the secrets of Sean's love life.

Lina rushed out and jumped around with her. "Congratulations! Let's celebrate!"

Mads and Lina left the theater and headed to Rutgers Street to celebrate her triumph. They went into Ike's Candy Store and picked out a big bag of jelly beans.

"You're an actress!" Lina cheered.

"Who cares?" Mads said. "Actress shmactress. Before you know it, I'll be friends with Jane Cotham, and soon I'll know every intimate detail about Sean! Maybe I'll even get to hang out with him after rehearsals."

"With Sean and Jane, you mean," Lina said. "And Stephen."

"Oh, yeah, Stephen." When Sean was in the picture,

Stephen had a tendency to fade away. It was as if she had two compartments in her mind, and in her heart. And they were very separate. "The important thing is, my master plan is working."

"What master plan?" Lina asked.

"Well, there's no actual plan," Mads admitted. "I kind of make it up as I go along. But I know the general direction I want to go in, and this takes me there."

9 Waaah!

To:	hollygolitely
From:	your daily horoscope

HERE IS TODAY'S HOROSCOPE: CAPRICORN: Do you know what a succubus is? No? Look it up. There's one headed your way.

Britta, what's the matter?"

Holly found Britta at her front door in tears.

"Come in," Holly said, pulling the sniffling girl inside and shutting the door. "My god, what happened? Are you hurt? Did someone die?"

Britta shook her head. "It's my parents. They're monsters! Fiends!"

"What did they do?"

"They're trying to stop me from seeing Ed!" Britta

cried. "They're worried that our relationship is too intense. They won't let me see him more than once a week—and he's leaving in less than three weeks! That means I'll only see him twice more before he leaves—and after that, who knows?"

She collapsed on Holly's shoulder and they both tumbled onto the couch in the great room. Luckily, Curt and Jen were at a country club dinner. It wouldn't be good for them to see this—Jen might report everything to Peggy Fowler.

"God, that's so unfair," Holly said. "Don't they understand what he means to you?"

Every day Britta gave Holly an Ed Report, and Holly was hooked on them. The flowers, the candles, the kisses, the poetry . . . It was all so romantic, like a dream. No one Holly knew had ever had a love affair—and that was what this was like, a grown-up, movie love affair—and Holly was enthralled by every detail.

"I know," Britta sobbed. "They're so mean! What am I going to do? My whole life has changed since I met him. Now I can't live without him!"

"Your parents are so overprotective," Holly said.

"Overprotective! All they care about are my grades and getting into Harvard. Superficial, status-conscious social climbers!"

Holly silently agreed. She thought of what Lina would say: What kind of cold-hearted people couldn't see true love when it bloomed like a desert cactus right in front of their eyes? And she'd be right. Holly wasn't about to let them quash it. It meant too much to Britta—and to Holly.

When Holly looked back on the relationships she'd had with boys so far, they all seemed kind of piddly. Ordinary, everyday. She'd felt attracted, she'd felt irritated, she'd felt pleasantly comfortable, she'd felt angry. But she'd never felt the huge emotions Britta had. She'd never felt like her love was a matter of life and death. And she wanted to. She was willing to make a sacrifice to keep Britta's love story going.

"Look, there's a very easy answer," Holly said. "You can see Ed whenever you want. Just tell Peggy and Gord that you're with me. I'll cover for you."

Britta lifted her head, sat up, and stared gratefully through her tears at Holly.

"You would do that for us?"

"Of course."

Britta started crying again. "Thank you . . . so much . . ."

Holly wrapped her arms around her and let her cry. A tear sprang up at the corner of her own eye. Ed and Britta needed her. Without Holly to protect it, their relationship would be trampled by a cruel world.

The doorbell rang. Holly got up to answer it, leaving Britta crumpled on the couch.

It was Rob. They were supposed to go out that night. In the midst of Britta's crisis, Holly had forgotten all about it.

"Hey," she said, kissing him lightly on the lips.

"Ready to go? I thought we could grab some Chinese food—" He came in and saw Britta on the couch. "What's up?" he asked, nodding at her.

"An emergency," Holly explained. "I can't leave her right now."

"Oh. What happened?"

"Her parents won't let her see Ed more than once a week," Holly said. "They're ruining her life!"

"Bummer." Holly could tell that Rob was trying to be sympathetic, but he really didn't get the implications of this. "Can we go out later, after she's calmed down?"

"I don't know." Holly led Rob over to the couch. Britta's face was buried in a cushion. "We'll see." She helped Britta up to a sitting position. "Would you like a glass of water?"

Britta nodded. Holly went to the kitchen. Rob followed her.

"How long do you think this is going to be?" Rob asked.

"I'm not sure," Holly said. "She's so in love, she takes everything to heart, you know?"

Rob didn't look too sure. Holly brought the glass of water to Britta. He followed her.

Britta drank the water and seemed to feel better. "Thanks, Holly. I guess everything is okay now, since you're going to help us. I'll call Ed and tell him what's going on." She pulled her cell phone out of her purse.

Holly and Rob stepped away so she could have some privacy. "Isn't it amazing?" Holly said. "I've never seen two people so in love. It's like this incredible Shakespearean super-love, like a fairy tale. Unreal."

Rob looked uncomfortable. "Unreal is a good word for it."

A few minutes later, Britta was off the phone, wailing. Holly and Rob ran to her.

"What is it?" Holly asked. "What's the matter now?"

"I'm—just—so—in—love—with—him," Britta choked out.

"Um, you know what? I think I'm going to go now," Rob said. He was practically squirming with discomfort. Holly felt sorry for him. Most boys, ordinary boys, couldn't handle this level of emotion.

"I'm sorry, Rob," she said, walking him to the door. "I can't leave her like this."

"I know. I'll call you later. Maybe we can catch a late movie? If she's gone by then, I mean."

"Okay." More wails issued from the couch. Holly turned her head.

"I'd better go." Rob left quickly. Holly hurried back to the couch.

"He's coming over," Britta said. "That's okay, isn't it?"

"Of course it is," Holly said. "But he's got to leave before Curt and Jen get home, or your parents will find out—"

"He will, he will."

"Britta, you've really got to stop crying now," Holly said. She grabbed a box of Kleenex and started dabbing at Britta's eyes. "There's nothing to cry about, right? Ed's coming over!"

Britta nodded happily. Holly helped her straighten her clothes in preparation for Ed's arrival. She felt like the nurse in Romeo and Juliet, helping the young lovers arrange a rendezvous. So much excitement, so much emotion. This wasn't high school. This was real life.

I hope this happens to me one day, Holly thought. She was happy to play nurse to Britta. But someday she wanted to be Juliet.

10 Naked Halloween

To:	linaonme
From:	your daily horoscope

HERE IS TODAY'S HOROSCOPE: CANCER: An irresistible opportunity presents itself today. Which is too bad for you, since resisting it is the only way to avoid catastrophe. But the stars say you won't, so I guess you're doomed.

L ina! This is it! The goddess is smiling down on us!"

Ramona was running down the hall toward her, waving a piece of paper. Lina sat on the floor in front of her locker, trying to squeeze in a last-minute cram for her history quiz. She closed her book. It was a lost cause now.

Ramona sat down next to her. "Look. It's the answer to everything."

Lina didn't have to ask what Ramona was talking about. What was Ramona always talking about? Or almost always? Dan.

Lina read the piece of paper. It was a flyer announcing Rosewood's annual Writer's Potluck Supper, for all students who write for school publications. This included Lina, of course, and Ramona, who was an editor and poet, specializing in death imagery, for *Inchworm*, one of the school's two literary journals. Lina was sure it would be somewhat fun, for a school party, but she didn't get what Ramona was so excited about.

"So?" Lina asked.

"Look where it's being held."

Lina read the smaller type at the bottom of the page. *Date, time, and address: the home of Dan Shulman*, Inchworm *Faculty Advisor.* Aha.

"There's got to be a way we can use this," Ramona said. "I mean, we're going to be *inside his house!* For a legitimate reason!"

"But what can we do?" Lina asked. "Chain ourselves to the bed?"

"I know—we'll steal something of his. And he'll have to ask you back to return it . . . No! We'll find his journal, or some personal letters or something, and blackmail him with them. He has to kiss you or we'll publish them on your Web site."

"That's horrible," Lina said. "Very mean. And it won't make him like me at all."

"You're right. It will make him hate you. Both of us. But what can we do? There's got to be something."

They sat quietly for a few minutes, thinking. Slowly a plan began to take shape in Lina's mind. *I'm really sick,* she thought as the hazy details gradually became clearer.

"I've got it," she said. "When the party is winding down, I'll hide in his bedroom closet. His bedroom has got to have a closet, right?"

"I'm liking this so far," Ramona said.

"Then, after everyone is gone, I'll come out. We'll be alone together. Maybe I'll offer to help him clean up."

"Which could lead to other things." Ramona nodded her head happily. "Like kissing . . . "

"It could work," Lina said. "Don't you think? I mean, it will be nighttime, we'll be alone together . . . anything could happen."

"Guess what? The Markowitzes said Mads can go to Stanford with Holly," Lina announced to her parents at dinner that night. With her Dan plan settled, it was time to attack her second problem—getting permission to go on the crazy college weekend.

"That doesn't surprise me," Sylvia Ozu said. They sat in the spare, minimalist dining room at a table too big for the three of them: Lina's father, Ken, at one end, her mother, Sylvia, at the other, and Lina marooned in the middle. It wasn't easy to pass dishes from one person to the next; you kind of had to stand up a little bit or slide the platter along the table with a push. Sylvia reached as far as her short arm would go for the bowl of green beans almondine. Lina helped her by giving the dish a shove.

"The Markowitzes are too lax with their children, I've always thought," Sylvia continued. "I mean, they're lovely people, very nice, but I wouldn't call them disciplinarians."

"Actually, they're pretty strict with Mads," Lina said. "Well, not strict exactly, but very protective. They worry a lot."

"That's not the same as setting out a clear set of rules and sticking with them," Sylvia said. "One look at their house tells you that."

Mads' house was messy, true. It was an eclectic jumble of stuff gathered over the years by every member of the family. They didn't seem to throw anything away. Lina's house was cool and modern, spare and very neat, with a faint Japanese influence. Lina preferred Mads' house.

"We're getting off track here, Sylvia," Ken said. "What difference does it make what the Markowitzes' house looks like? The question is, Can Lina go away for the weekend with her two best friends?"

Thank you, Dad. Sylvia, an allergist, was a little chilly and could be stern with Lina. But Ken, a banker, usually took Lina's side. Still, even Lina and Ken teamed up together could rarely defeat a determined Sylvia.

"Ken, do you remember what you were like in college?" Sylvia said. "Do you remember how you spent your weekends? Do you really think Lina is ready to be exposed to that?"

Ken scratched his chin as if trying to summon up the memory. "I remember having a hell of a lot of fun," he said.

"You were a lacrosse player," Sylvia reminded him. "They were *the worst*."

Ken laughed. "What about you? The theater crowd?"

"I was pre-med."

"But all your friends were theater kids. Your parties were notorious! Remember 'Naked Halloween'?"

Lina's ears perked up. Naked Halloween? Sylvia?

Sylvia looked annoyed. "You're only proving my point—a college campus is no place for a fifteen-year-old girl."

"What's Naked Halloween?" Lina asked.

Sylvia shot her a freeze-glare, but Ken said, "It was a big costume party where everyone was supposed to come as a ghost—only you had to be naked under the sheet."

"Mom? You did that?"

"No, I did not. I always wore a flesh-colored leotard under my sheet," Sylvia said.

"Once the party got going people tried to rip each other's sheets off," Ken explained.

"And anyway, I secretly attached my sheet to my waist, so you couldn't pull it off if you tried," Sylvia said.

"And believe me, people tried," Ken said.

"It was barbaric," Sylvia said.

"Hey, that was your crowd," Ken said. "We didn't stoop that low at Toad Hall." Toad Hall was the name of Ken's lacrosse fraternity. Lina had heard a few wild stories about their parties, too.

"Toad Hall was a slime pit," Sylvia said. "Lina, pass the fish."

That was her signal that the subject was closed. Lina passed the fish. They ate in silence for a few minutes, flatware clicking against china.

Lina and Ken traded surreptitious glances while Sylvia focused on her plate. "More water, Lina?" Ken asked, standing up to fill her glass from a pitcher. He gave her a little wink. She took this as a signal. *I've softened her up.*

You take it from here.

"It's so interesting to hear you two talk about your college days," Lina said. "Do you know what I've learned from this? I've learned that a person with strong character, a good family, raised with the right values, can withstand almost any temptation or corruption. Just look at what you both went through at college—the decadence! And see how well you turned out? Moral, upstanding citizens. And you raised me to be that way, too. It will take more than a wild frat party to change that."

She was afraid to peek at Sylvia's face—did that snow her? But she couldn't resist. Sylvia didn't look up. She chewed on a bean. She took a sip of water. She kept her eyes focused on the gleaming wooden table.

Aha, Lina thought. *She doesn't want to look up at us because she knows once she does it's all over.*

Sylvia swallowed. She looked up. First at Ken, then Lina.

"I still think you're too young," she said.

"It's only a weekend, Sylvia," Ken said. "Piper Anderson will look out for them."

"That's what I'm afraid of," Sylvia said. She turned to Lina. "If I let you go, will you leave you cell phone on *the entire time* so we can check on you at any moment, day or night?"

"Yes! I promise," Lina said.

"Do you know what will happen if your cell phone rings and you don't answer it?"

"Grounded for eternity?" Lina guessed.

"Correct. And do you know what will happen if we call you and you answer in a compromising position or some state of intoxication?"

"Death by scolding?"

"Or worse." Sylvia paused, just for dramatic effect. She had once run with the theater crowd, after all.

"All right. You may go."

linaonme: guess what? I can go to stanford!

hollygolitely: sylvia actually said yes?

linaonme: 10-4. And wait till you hear what she used to do in college. I'll tell u tomorrow at school.

mad4u: so it's all settled? We're all going now?

hollygolitely: all settled.

mad4u: yay!

linaonme: this is going to be so much fun! The crazy college weekend is on!

11 Jane Starts Talking

| To: | mad4u |
| From: | your daily horoscope |

HERE IS TODAY'S HOROSCOPE: VIRGO: You got yourself into this mess. What are you looking at me for?

El Diario

To my dear loyal readers,
Never act in a play written by your own mother. In fact, if your mother expresses any interest in writing a play, do everything you can to stop her. And if she manages to get some words on paper, destroy them!

"Someday, little Mariah, you're going to grow up and marry a farmer just like your Papa." A woman named

Kendall, who played Mama in *Touched*, was reading from the script. The whole cast was assembled for a read-through of the play. Mads thought Kendall didn't look much like anyone's Mama, with her spiky crimson hair and clanky jewelry, but she figured costumes and makeup would take care of that.

"No, Mama," Audrey read. "Papa is a good man. But I won't spend my life toiling in the soil. I want to be FREE AS A BUTTERFLY!" Audrey's voice rose to a screech and she flung her arm in the air.

"All right, Audrey, good," Charles Huang, the director, said. "But you don't have to scream at the end of the line. Just say it like you normally would. Try it again."

"The problem is nobody normal would say a line like that." Damien Chopra, who played Buck, Mariah's first love, leaned close to Jane and whispered those words. Mads, who was sitting on Jane's other side, overheard them. She couldn't agree more.

Jane glanced at Mads as if worried they'd offended her. The woman who wrote those words was Mads' mother, after all. They probably assumed she thought the play was great. Mads would have to set them straight as soon as she could. She smiled and nodded to let them know she was on their side. Jane turned away.

From the beginning, Jane had been aloof. Mads was

starting to think Jane would never confide anything to her. But if she didn't, Mads was putting herself through this torture for nothing, and that was too terrible to think about.

"I want to be free—as a butterfly." This time Audrey whispered the end of the sentence.

"Um, okay, let's take a fifteen-minute break," Charles said.

The cast noisily pushed their chairs from the table. M.C. came up to Mads and Audrey and hugged them. "Isn't this is exciting? It's so exciting! People are actually speaking the words that I wrote! I can't stand it!"

She ran after Charles to ask him something. The grin on her face looked tense and frozen.

"Bet you twenty bucks she cracks by opening night," Mads said.

"You're on," Audrey said. "Mama!" she called, running after M.C. Both M.C. and Kendall turned around.

"So that's your little sister, huh," Damien said.

"Yep," Mads said.

"And M.C.'s your mom?"

"That's what it says on my birth certificate."

"They're cool. So what happened to you?" Mads was startled for a second—who was he to insult her? He hardly knew her. But the grin on his face told her he was just joking around. "Guess you take after your dad."

"At least my parents didn't name me after a psycho," Mads teased, thinking of an old movie she once saw about a crazed kid named Damien.

"No, they just named you after a president. Or an avenue. Or a basketball arena in New York."

"What's wrong with that?"

"Better watch out," Damien said. "They named me Damien for a reason." He made a face and pretended to grab at her neck. Instead he tickled her, and Mads laughed.

"You all ready for our big lip-lock, Teen Mariah?" he asked. Damien was cute, a college freshman, but he could pass for younger. So he was playing both Teen Buck and Grown-up Buck. Mads would have to kiss him at the end of Act I. Looking him over, she decided not to mind.

"I'm ready, but can you handle it, Buck?" she said.

"Don't worry about me. I've got the kissing thing *down*," Damien said.

"Madison?" Jane came over to them. "Don't take offense but I think your mother is losing it already."

She pointed into the wings, where M.C. was hyperventilating and Charles was helping her sit down. M.C. leaned against the curtain, breathing easier now.

"Is everything all right?" Jane said.

"She's just the anxious type," Mads said.

"I'll say," Jane said. "And what's with your sister? Act much?"

Jane clearly had no fear of offending Mads anymore. Mads decided to take it as a sign of confidence in her. Straight talk.

"She's a big ham. We're just lucky the theater isn't doing a musical. *Annie* would be especially deadly," Mads said.

"I know the type," Jane said. "My boyfriend is a big show-off. He'll do almost anything for attention."

Aha. This was what Mads had signed on for. Although she already knew Sean liked attention. But it was interesting to hear Jane say it this way. Almost as if she were putting him down. Just a little.

"Really?" Mads said, as if she didn't know.

"Oh yeah. He's got copies of every video his mother ever shot of him, lined up in chronological order on his bookcase. If you go to his house he makes you watch them. It's pretty funny. Here's little Sean getting potty-trained, here's little Sean learning to swim, here's little Sean modeling his new school clothes . . ."

"Talk about ego," Damien said.

"He's not embarrassed about it at all," Jane said. "I mean, he has no sense of irony. It's endearing, in a way."

"Till you get tired of it," Damien said.

"And he's superstitious," Jane said. "Do you know that on the day of a swim meet he *has* to wear these goofy boxer shorts with candy canes on them? Because he wore them the day he won some big meet. If he can't wear them he goes crazy. But they're worn to shreds. There's a big hole in the back. . . ."

Wow, Mads thought. Imagine knowing Sean so well you knew that he had a hole in his underwear. She tried to think of something she could say about Stephen, something intimate like that. But she didn't know him that well yet.

Damien was laughing, and Mads couldn't help wondering if some of this talk was for his benefit. Jane seemed to be making gentle fun of a boy she cared about, but in another way it was as if she were roasting him and serving him up to be attacked by Damien. Like she was sending Damien a secret message: Yes, I date the very hot Sean (of course, because I'm so beautiful), but that doesn't mean he's not vulnerable to a hostile takeover. Or that I'm not open to a friendly one.

"My boyfriend is actually kind of quiet," Mads said. "He's not very attention-grabby at all. Although he did make a big splash at the art fair, so I guess he doesn't *mind* attention. . . ."

"That guy is your boyfriend?" Jane asked. "The one

who did the giant installation of a bedroom?" Mads nodded. "That was cool. There's something about that guy. He's kind of sexy," Jane said.

Mads clenched her teeth to keep her jaw from dropping open in shock. Jane thought Stephen was sexy? Sean's girlfriend thought Mads' boyfriend was sexy? Stephen suddenly gained a new stature in Mads' imagination. A golden aura glowed around him. Not as strong as Sean's, but it was there. He was sexy. If Jane thought so, it had to be true.

mad4u: guess what jane told me today? Sean wears boxer shorts with candy canes on them! and a big hole in the back!

linaonme: gross.

mad4u: where's holly? I can't wait 2 tell her.

linaonme: don't know. I tried to call her a while ago but she was out.

mad4u: I want 2 write about the stuff jane said in my blog diary—but what if sean reads it? he might get mad.

linaonme: use fake names. Like the blind items in a gossip column.

mad4u: hmmm . . . maybe. But sean will still know it's him.

linaonme: but he'll never admit it, so he won't tell anyone. except maybe jane. He might get mad at her.

mad4u: that might be good . . . can't decide. What have u
been up 2?

linaonme: ramona and I made a plan to get dan. After the
writers dinner I hide in his closet and come out when
everyone's gone. What do u think?

mad4u: interesting. Wacky, yet clever. If it doesn't backfire.

linaonme: there's always that.

mad4u: what r u doing 2nite?

llinaonme: nothing. Walker asked me to go to the movies but I
told him I had 2 much homework.

mad4u: the movies? Was it a date?

linaonme: no. just a friend thing. with a group. But now that
we're talking about movies, I feel like going out. kiss me
stinky!

mad4u: I'm dying to see it. let's go 2nite. I'll call holly.

Holly wasn't online, so Mads tried her cell. She got
voice mail. She tried Holly at home and Jen answered.

"Hi, honey," Jen said. "Holly's not here. She's out with
Britta tonight."

Britta again? Mads said, "Thanks, Jen," and hung up.
Then she dialed Lina.

"Holly's not home. She's doing something with
Britta."

"Are you kidding me?" Lina said. "She's always with

Britta. We were supposed to get together after school yesterday but she canceled on me to help Britta shop for a new dress."

"Oh, right—because Ed was taking her to Le Mas for their two-week anniversary." Le Mas was a very romantic, fancy restaurant in an old farmhouse just outside of town. "I wish Stephen would take me there, but it's so expensive."

Lina sighed. "My parents took me there once. It's beautiful, but you don't want to be there with your parents."

"Britta is so lucky," Mads said. "But I wish she wouldn't hog Holly so much."

"I really want to see that movie tonight," Lina said.

"Me, too," Mads said. "But we promised Holly we'd see it with her."

"How can we if she's always busy with Britta? She can see it with Britta if she wants," Lina said.

"I guess," Mads said. "It's not so terrible if we go without her, is it?"

"No one is keeping her from seeing the movie," Lina said.

"Okay," Mads said. "Let's go."

12 The Love Nest

To:	hollygolitely
From:	your daily horoscope

HERE IS TODAY'S HOROSCOPE: CAPRICORN: If you wear sticky-sweet perfume, you attract sticky-sweet people.

I know it's dark out, but we can't turn on the flashlight until we get inside," Ed whispered. He led Holly, Rob, and Britta through the dark down a stone path to a small beach house. The nearest house was a quarter of a mile away, but Ed didn't want them to be seen from the road.

Holly stumbled on a rock and fell against Rob, who put his arm around her. In his other hand he carried a cooler full of food and drinks. Ed carried a pizza. Holly and Rob were double-dating with Britta and Ed, and Britta had suggested showing them their secret hideaway.

The door was unlocked. Once inside the house Ed turned on his flashlight. The electricity had been shut off. It was spooky. All the shades were drawn on the roadside windows, but the seaside part of the house was open to the water. Holly could hear the waves lapping on the shore.

Britta bustled around lighting candles and lanterns. "Isn't it beautiful?" she said.

"It's so sweet," Holly said. "Like a playhouse for grown-ups." The house was unfurnished, but Britta and Ed had made a low table out of bricks and a board and set out a thick blanket on the floor with cushions to sit on. They had a boom box for music. There were ashes in the fireplace; it had obviously been used very recently. And spread out near the fireplace was another blanket and some pillows, set up like a bed. They had made the house their own. It was bare but so cozy. Holly felt as if she were in a fairy tale cottage in an enchanted forest.

Britta kept a stack of plastic plates and cups and knives and forks under the makeshift table. Ed opened a bottle of wine. Holly admired the way they each knew what to do without having to speak. They were one unit, a real couple. *It must feel so nice,* she thought.

Ed set the bottle on the low table. He leaned across it and kissed Britta, long and slow and deeply. Their faces were illuminated by the candles. Holly stared for a second; she felt as if she were watching a romantic movie. But then she remembered this was real and maybe she shouldn't stare. She glanced at Rob. He was looking at his hands in his lap, where he was trying to wage a thumb war with himself. His left thumb was severely handicapped, however, since he was a righty.

"Who wants pizza?" Britta finally disengaged herself and asked.

"I do," Rob said. "I'm starving."

They gathered on cushions around the table. Britta put some soft music on the box. They couldn't make too much noise or they might get caught.

Britta gleamed in the candlelight. Her hair was tied back with a scarf, and she wore mascara, lipstick, and a low-cut blouse. Holly couldn't get over it. Every time she saw Britta she seemed more womanly and more beautiful. She caught Ed staring at Britta with admiration in his eyes. Britta looked back at him and flushed. Holly reached for Rob's hand. Thumb war over. It was time for love.

With his free hand Rob lifted the top of the pizza box. "So, what kind did we get? Looks like half-mushroom, half-pepperoni. Excellent. Half-mush, half-pep, we call it at my house." He took a pepperoni slice and plopped it onto his plate. "What kind do you want, Holly?"

Holly was watching Ed and Britta gaze into each other's eyes. Ed obviously didn't care about food—all he cared about was Britta. Holly wondered what it felt like to have a boy look at you that way, as if you were the most beautiful person in the world.

"Holly? You're a mushroom girl, usually," Rob said. He gave Holly a slice of mushroom. "Ed? Britta? You eating?"

Ed dragged his eyes away from Britta's face to look at Rob, then the pizza. "What would you like, love?" He had a faint English accent.

"Wait—" Britta picked up a slice of mushroom. "Here." She held the dripping pizza for him and fed him a bite. A string of mozzarella stretched between his teeth and the slice, then snapped and landed on his chin. Britta gently plucked it off and popped it into his mouth. They were so intimate with each other. Holly longed to have that same feeling with Rob. At least he knew what kind of pizza she liked. Ed served a slice to Britta and they started eating.

"Don't you love this house?" Holly said to Rob. "It's so cozy, even without electricity." He nodded.

"I hope no one ever buys it," Britta said. "I feel like it's ours. I hate to think of some family moving in here and bickering over what TV show to watch or yelling at their kids to do their homework. You know? It would drive out the love vibe."

"The love vibe?" Rob said. "What are you talking about? You don't want the people who live here to watch TV? If you lived here long enough, you'd get around to watching TV at some point, I bet."

"I know what you mean, Britta," Holly said. "This house shouldn't have to see petty, everyday problems. It's a love house."

"That reminds me." Ed rummaged through his backpack until he found a package wrapped in tissue paper. "Britta, I made this for you. I didn't mean to give it to you in front of anyone else, but . . . well, I think your friends will understand. I can't wait to see how you like it."

Britta tore off the paper. Inside was a framed drawing of the house they were all sitting in at that moment, styled so it looked even more like a sweet, cozy cottage than it really was. Smoke curled out of the chimney, a dog slept peacefully on the front step, and the welcome mat read "Bless Our House and Its Heart So Savage."

"Oh, Ed, it's beautiful," Britta said. "You made this? I didn't even know you could draw." She studied it again, and tears sprang to her eyes. "It looks as if we live here. Or at least someone very happy lives here." She put the picture on the table and they kissed again, a good three minutes this time.

Rob picked up the picture and stared at it. "'Heart So Savage'? What's that supposed to mean?" he whispered to Holly.

"Like, true love," Holly said. "Fierce and passionate. Like a wild animal."

Rob made a face. "This guy is too much," he whispered.

Holly felt sad. Why couldn't Rob see the beauty of all this? He'd never be passionate with her the way Ed was with Britta, not if he thought it was all silly.

They finished the pizza. It was a warm night so they didn't light a fire. They all sat on the deck watching the moon set over the water and slapping mosquitoes away.

"It feels like we're in another world," Holly sighed. "Far away from our real lives. In a story, or a movie."

No one said anything. Holly heard a faint lapping sound. Britta and Ed were furiously making out.

Rob reached for Holly in the dark and kissed her lightly. "Can we get out of here now?"

"Oh, already?" Holly said. She loved the little house. She didn't want to leave. And she was hoping it would work its magic on Rob somehow, if they just stayed long enough.

"I'm getting restless," Rob said. "Let's go for a drive."

"Okay." A drive wasn't so bad. On a warm, moonlit

night, it was kind of romantic. They got to their feet. Ed
and Britta were so busy making out they didn't notice.

Rob cleared his throat. "We're out of here," he said.
"Thanks for pizza and everything."

"Thanks for letting us see the house," Holly said. "I
really love it."

Ed and Britta disengaged again and got up. "You're
welcome," Britta said. "Maybe next time we can all go for
a midnight swim."

"Be careful in the dark out there," Ed said. They
walked Rob and Holly to the door, and stood framed in
the candlelight, arm-in-arm, watching them go.

Holly and Rob picked their way along the path until
they got to Rob's SUV. Holly glanced back at the house.
From the street you could see only the slightest trace of
light in the windows. If you weren't looking for it you'd
never notice someone was inside. It was like a secret world
that disappeared as soon as you stepped away.

"Can we not double with them again?" Rob asked.

"What?" Holly said. "But they're so sweet together.
And it's Britta's first love; I feel as if I need to make sure it
goes okay."

"It's going fine without you, trust me," Rob said.

"Ed won't be here much longer," Holly said. "I think
that's why they're so obsessed with each other. They're

trying to squeeze everything they can into a few weeks." But it wasn't just that that Holly envied; it was the seriousness between them. They weren't boyfriend and girlfriend; they were lovers.

"Well, I can't wait until that dude leaves," Rob said. "You're too involved in this whole thing. You spend too much time with Britta."

"Why do you say that? I spend a lot of time with Mads and Lina too, and that never bothered you."

"They're different," Rob said. "They don't shut me out when I'm around. Britta shuts out everyone but Ed. And he does the same thing. I feel like they don't really want us around."

"They do, I know they do," Holly said. "Britta always says so. And look how much good it's done her. Do you remember what she used to be like?"

"Yeah. Geek city."

"And now?"

"Like a big drip. If you ask me," Rob said.

"She looks gorgeous! The love is just shining out from her skin."

Rob shrugged. "Give me a good old-fashioned geek any day."

She knew he didn't mean that. "I feel like I have to help her," Holly said. "She's never had a boyfriend before.

She's never been through any of this stuff before. And her parents are always worrying about every little thing. . . . She needs someone on her side."

"They creep me out," Rob said. "They're too intense. Always licking each other and staring into each other's eyes."

"I don't think it's creepy," Holly said. "I think it's beautiful. It's true love."

"No," Rob said. "This is true love." He stopped the car at a red light and brushed Holly's hair from her face. Then he kissed her forehead, her nose, each cheek, and her mouth, in a kind of cross. "See? I can be Mr. Casanova, too," he said. "When I want to be."

Holly loved the kisses—but Rob ruined the mood with his comment. Did he mean what he said about true love? Maybe, but even so, Holly was afraid he didn't quite get it.

QUIZ: IS YOUR RELATIONSHIP TOO INTENSE?
There's good intense and bad intense.
Do you know the difference?

1   On the first date he takes you to:

a ▶ a movie

b ▶ an expensive dinner

c ▶ Paris

d ▶ couples counseling

2 You meet his parents. They say:

a▶ "Nice to meet you."

b▶ "What a sweet girl."

c▶ "Do you want a church wedding or justice of the peace?"

d▶ "She'll be a nice addition to the bloodline."

3 He says he doesn't want to see you too often, only:

a▶ once a month

b▶ once a week

c▶ once a day

d▶ once an hour

4 His nickname for you is:

a▶ honey

b▶ sweetie

c▶ soul-baby

d▶ mother-of-my-children

5 When your parents met him their reaction was:

a▶ polite

b▶ pleased

c▶ overjoyed

d▶ they took out a restraining order

6   He runs out to the store to get ice cream. You feel:

a ▶ impatient—you're hungry

b ▶ nothing—he'll be back before you know it

c ▶ edgy—what's taking him so long?

d ▶ panic—by the time he returns twenty minutes later, you've already composed a suicide note because you can't live without him

7   You love him because:

a ▶ he's sexy

b ▶ he's good to you

c ▶ he needs you so much

d ▶ without him you're nothing

Scoring: If you picked any d's, your relationship is intense to the point of sickness! You need help. More than two c's signal trouble, too. Otherwise, you're probably okay.

"I talked to Peggy Fowler last night while you all were out," Jen said at breakfast the next morning. Curt had already left for work. Jen sat with a cup of black coffee, tapping her fingers on the table, jonesing for a cigarette. She'd quit smoking five years before, but she was born a smoker and would always be a smoker, even if she never took another puff.

"Yeah?" Holly spooned a slice of grapefruit into her

mouth. She had a feeling that whatever was coming next wasn't good.

"Well, she's worried," Jen said. "You know how they are. I try to tell her to calm down, be more like me and your father. You and Piper are turning out okay, and we don't get all worked up about what you're up to." She paused for a sip of coffee. "But you're not up to anything bad, are you?"

"No, Jen," Holly said. "Nothing you wouldn't do."

"That's not the best answer I could hear, but I'll take it," Jen said. "This thing with Britta does sound a little funny, though. It's like in an old movie when the heroine takes off her glasses and lets down her hair, and suddenly she's a whole different person. I can't blame Peggy for worrying. She says Britta is obsessed. She doesn't care about anything anymore unless it has to do with that boy. What's his name?"

"Ed."

"Ed. Who falls in love with an Ed? She hardly eats, she hardly studies, Peg practically has to kick her out of bed in the mornings and force her to go to school. . . . And she was always such a nerd!"

"She's changing," Holly said. "Life is opening up to her. She's like Jane Eyre after she falls in love with Rochester. I think it's a good thing. It's normal! I've had crushes like this before. I just never let you in on it."

"Really? I don't remember ever seeing you not eat."

"Very funny. Britta's just getting more normal. Peggy's not used to that after all these years raising a nerd. There's nothing to worry about. I'm sure."

"What makes you so smart?" Jen asked. "You talk to me as if I were one of your friends, not your mother."

"Jen, think about it," Holly said.

Jen didn't bother. "I guess you're right," Jen said. "I've never been very maternal, have I?"

"No," Holly said. She got up, put her bowl in the sink, and gave her mother a kiss. "And that's the way I like it."

13 Kiss Me, Stinky

To:	mad4u
From:	your daily horoscope

HERE IS TODAY'S HOROSCOPE: VIRGO: If knowledge is power, you are about to be handed a neutron bomb.

I loved the part when she comes home to meet her new roommate and the apartment looks like a tornado ripped through it," Mads said. She and Lina walked out of the movie theater after a showing of *Kiss Me, Stinky*. The movie was even better than Mads had hoped.

"I liked the part at the end when she kisses him even though he's covered in garbage," Lina said. She tossed her popcorn bag in the trash. "Ew. But I would have kissed him, too."

The Carlton Bay Twin had two theaters, and both movies had let out at the same time. The crowd milled about on the sidewalk in front of the theater, clogging the lobby. Mads caught a glimpse of short, spiky brown hair in the crowd. It belonged to Walker Moore. He spotted her and smiled. Then he saw Lina and his smile disappeared.

"Hi, Walker," Mads said, elbowing Lina to give her as much time as possible to prepare a decent lie.

"Hi, Mads. Hi, *Lina*," he said in a pointed way.

"Hey, Walker." Lina didn't seem disturbed by this sighting in the least. Mads thought that was strange. Hadn't Walker asked her to the movies that night? And hadn't Lina told him that she had too much homework to go? So hadn't she just been caught in a lie? Wasn't she afraid Walker would be hurt, or angry?

"We just saw *Kiss Me, Stinky*," Lina said. "It rocked!"

"Really?" Walker looked confused. "I saw *Rocket to Russia*."

"How was it?" Lina asked.

"Good," Walker said.

"Who did you see it with?" Lina asked.

"Nobody," Walker said.

"Oh," Lina said.

"I thought you had too much homework to go to the movies," Walker said.

"I was going to do some homework, but then—"

"—I called her up and *begged* her to come to the movies with me," Mads said. "I wouldn't take no for an answer. Right, Lina?"

"Actually, *I* was the one—"

"That's okay," Walker said, but it didn't look okay to Mads. "You don't need to give me an excuse."

He walked away, long loping strides, his hands shoved in his jacket pockets.

"Mads, why did you lie like that?" Lina asked.

"Well, he seemed kind of upset," Mads said. "I mean, you told him you had too much homework—"

"Why should he be upset?" Lina said. "If you went to the movies without me, I wouldn't care. Unless we planned to go together, like tonight. But I never had a plan with Walker."

"I guess," Mads said, but something didn't feel right about it.

"Don't worry, Mads," Lina said. "He doesn't care. We're friends."

"All right, Madison, that was good," Charles said. Mads had just finished rehearsing a scene with "Mama," or Kendall. She had actually managed to remember all her lines this time, which was a first. She was starting to like this acting thing. "I just want you to think about ESP and how it feels. You don't happen to have ESP, do you?"

Mads shook her head. "M.C. has it, but I don't think I got that gene."

"Too bad. Well, talk to her about what it feels like and think about how you might show that with your body. Without going overboard or being hokey. Okey-dokey?"

"Okay," Mads said, but it sounded impossible.

"Take a break," Charles said. "I need everyone from Act One, scene three, on stage now!"

Audrey flounced past Mads; this was her cue. "I can really see that zit on your forehead under the stage lights," she said to Mads. "I've got makeup in my backpack if you want to borrow some."

Mads' hand flew to her forehead. Whatever that was up there felt huge, the size of a lima bean. "What are you doing with makeup?" she demanded. "You're too young."

"I need it. I'm an actress now."

"Oh, please." But she wandered through the wings, looking for Audrey's backpack. She couldn't walk around with a neon-red zit blaring on her forehead. She finally found the backpack tossed behind a large box. She unzipped it and started rifling through all Audrey's junk. You'd think she'd have a few school books in there, Mads thought—they had just come from school—but no. The bag was full of hair clips and scrunchies, an extra pair of shoes and an extra top, a small stuffed kitty, several mysterious pink plastic zippered cases, crumpled-up notes from friends, and makeup. Mads was just pulling the concealer out when she heard someone nearby giggle and say "Shh!"

Mads instinctively froze. Why, she couldn't say. She wasn't doing anything wrong. But if somebody else was, she wanted to find out about it. And they might stop doing it if they knew she was there.

The giggling came from behind a curtain a few feet away from Mads. "We'd better go back and watch rehearsal," a guy's voice whispered. "Charles is calling one of my scenes next."

Damien, Mads thought. But who was he with?

"Shh! Just be quiet for one second."

Jane! What was she doing?

As quietly as she could, Mads slid across the dusty wooden floor on her butt. She could just see Jane and Damien huddled in the folds of a heavy stage curtain. Jane pulled Damien toward her and gave him a long, slow kiss.

Oh my god! Mads bit her tongue to keep from gasping. Jane—Sean's girlfriend Jane—was kissing Damien! And it wasn't as if he were forcing himself on her and she was resisting. This kiss was definitely her idea.

"Act One, scene four!" Charles called from the auditorium.

"That's me," Damien said, pulling away from Jane. He leaned forward for a last peck on the lips and hurried on stage.

Mads scuttled back to Audrey's backpack and made herself look busy, in case anybody spotted her. She glanced back and saw Jane languidly walk toward the stage to watch Damien's scene.

She's cheating on Sean, Mads thought. The idea took a while to sink in. How could anyone cheat on Sean? When your boyfriend was the hottest guy for miles around—*way hotter than Damien,* Mads thought, though he had his charms—why would you want to kiss someone else? Mads couldn't get her mind around it.

Should I do something? What should I do? she wondered. *Should I tell Sean?*

No, she thought at first. *That's too mean. Too tattletale-y.*

But her imagination began to run away with her. How would Sean react if he knew Jane was unfaithful to him? In her mind she saw a scene, as real as any in the play. She gently, hesitantly tells Sean what she has seen. She tries to play it down and say it was probably nothing. But Sean is hurt, then angry. Then hurt again, so sad . . . he needs someone to console him, to comfort him, and

Mads just happens to be right in front of him. He reaches for her, tears brimming in his eyes . . . *You would never do something like that, would you?* he asks, leaning down to kiss Mads. One thing leads to another . . .

Man, Mads thought. *That would be worth almost anything.*

Jane was the one acting like a slut, after all, she reasoned. Mads didn't force her to kiss Damien. But Sean should know about it. Otherwise, he was living a lie! And he really shouldn't be doing that.

All I'd be doing is telling the truth, Mads thought. *That's supposed to be a good thing, right? If Jane pays a price for it, well, that's what happens when you go around kissing every cute guy who crosses your path.*

That decided it. Mads was going to tell Sean the first chance she got. Jane was toast.

14 Here Comes the Bride

HERE IS TODAY'S HOROSCOPE: CAPRICORN: Well, well, well. Satisfied?

Britta? Why are you crying?"

Britta had arrived on Holly's doorstep in tears again. She was so emotional, up, down, a regular roller coaster. Not that Holly blamed her; that was love for you. True love, anyway. As illustrated by Britta and Ed, at least.

"Oh, Holly, I can't stand it!" Britta sobbed. Holly hustled her inside and up to her room. "It's almost over! In a week he'll be gone!"

"Back to England?" Holly asked.

Britta nodded. "I don't know what I'll do. I feel like . . . like . . . my life will be over! Kill me now!"

Holly held Britta, who was crying so hard she soaked Holly's shirt. "Shh, shh," Holly said, trying to soothe her. "Your life won't be over. He'll come back. And you can write him. . . . " But Holly knew that wasn't the same.

"I don't have a life! Not without him." Britta sobbed so violently Holly thought she could hear her heart actually breaking. She wanted to cry, too. It was so sad! But she had to stay strong for Britta.

"Think about what my life was like before," Britta said when she'd calmed down a little. "Sheer emptiness! Lessons and practices and studying and blah blah blah. It wasn't even a life."

Holly remembered. That was what had motivated her to fix Britta up in the first place. But now Britta had the most exciting life of anyone she knew. Sure there were lows, but the highs were so high, and even the sad times were kind of beautiful, in a tragic way. Holly understood how Britta felt—it would be devastating when Ed left. But she had to try to make her feel better, even if she knew it was hopeless.

"You can e-mail Ed, and write love letters to him," Holly said. "And he'll be back sometime, won't he?"

"Not until Thanksgiving," Britta wailed. "At the earliest."

"Well, maybe you can go visit him in London," Holly said. "This summer! That would be romantic . . ."

"My parents will never let me," Britta said. "I'm supposed to spend this summer working in a research lab." She flopped back on Holly's bed, wiping the tears away from her blotchy red face. "You know, a few weeks ago I was actually looking forward to it. Looking forward to spending the summer cooped up in a laboratory like a rat. It's pathetic."

"Well, maybe you'll meet someone cute there," Holly said. "I bet you'll find a great guy this summer, and things will be fun again. You can even take him to your beach house."

Britta stared at Holly as if she had said she liked to kidnap puppies, boil them up, and eat them on toast.

"There will never be anyone like Ed," she said solemnly. "No one can ever replace him. And I would never take some strange guy into *our* house."

"I know, I'm sorry," Holly said, backing away. Boiled puppies on toast, anyone?

Britta was calm now, steely and determined. "Ed was right," she said quietly.

"Right about what?" Holly asked.

"He said we should get married, the day after I met him," Britta said.

Holly was amazed. Ed proposed marriage after knowing Britta one day? "Wow, that's incredible," Holly said.
"He must really love you."

Marriage! This was Holly's greatest matchmaking
coup ever. Of course, she didn't actually fix up Britta with
Ed, but she did try to fix her up with somebody, anybody,
and it all happened because of Holly.

"He said it was the only way we could be together,"
Britta said. "And it is. I'm going to do it. I'm going to
marry him."

"Well, yeah," Holly said. "You two will get married
for sure one day. I've never seen a couple so made for
each other."

"No," Britta said. "Not one day. Now."

"Now?" Holly wasn't sure she'd heard right. Britta
wanted to get married? Now? At seventeen? In the middle
of junior year?

"Why not?" Britta said. "I want to be with Ed every
possible minute. My life is meaningless without him. The
only way I can stay with him is if I marry him before he
leaves. Then I can go to England with him. And we'll find
a little English cottage all our own."

"Wait a second. You want to marry him before he
leaves? Like, by Monday?" Holly was shocked, but as the
idea washed over her she saw what Britta meant. It was

inevitable. Britta and Ed had to stay together any way they could. For them, being apart would just be wrong.

"There's no other way out," Britta said. "If I don't, I might as well just lie down and die."

"Married," Holly said, letting the word linger on her tongue. "How will you do it?"

"We'll elope," Britta said. "We've talked about it before." Holly pictured Ed and Britta snuggling by the fire in the little beach house, planning their secret wedding. "I'll sneak out one night and he'll meet me at the end of the block. We'll spend the night together, and the next morning we'll drive to Las Vegas or someplace and get married. Once it's done, my parents won't be able to do anything about it. Maybe I won't even come home. I'll just fly off to England from there, and call my parents from the airport to say good-bye."

"It's like a movie," Holly said. "Did you ever see *True Romance*? It's like that without the killing spree." Holly paused. They weren't planning a killing spree, were they? No, this was Britta and Ed.

Britta squeezed Holly's hands. "Listen—I'm going to do this. I'm going to marry him. But you can't tell my parents. Or yours. Or *anyone*. Do you promise?"

"Yes, okay. I promise."

"Because if my parents find out they'll lock me up like

Rapunzel in the tower. And my hair's not long enough to make a ladder to the ground—even from a second-story window. So you promise? You swear?"

"I swear," Holly said. But as she said the words, an image of Britta's parents appeared in her mind. It was like that scene in *The Wizard of Oz*, when the Wicked Witch shows Dorothy her Aunt Em in the crystal ball. Auntie Em is calling for Dorothy and crying, *Where are you?* . . . The Fowlers would be crushed. Holly knew that. But on the other hand, Britta needed to be with Ed. If they were separated, she'd wilt back into the old, dull Britta, only half-alive. And wasn't that important, too?

"You swear on all that's good and beautiful in the world?" Britta pressed.

"Yes," Holly said. "I promise. I won't tell anyone."

15 Pot Luck

HERE IS TODAY'S HOROSCOPE: CANCER: Um, are you crazy?

I hope you're wearing something good," Ramona said as she and Lina stood on the threshold of Dan Shulman's one-story bungalow. "I mean underneath that sack."

"What? You don't like it?" Lina glanced down at the simple navy blue shift dress she had picked out to wear to the Rosewood Writers Potluck. She'd borrowed it from her mother, so maybe it was a little big, but she thought it looked sophisticated. She added a string of pearls and put her hair up for even more adultivity. "Should I go home and change?"

"Too late for that now. I just hope you're wearing lingerie underneath. That's what counts." Ramona shifted the salad she'd brought to one arm and rang the doorbell. Lina peered through the plastic wrap into Ramona's bowl. Inside was a pile of what looked like some kind of weird weed Ramona had dug out of the grass. Lina thought she still saw some dirt clinging to some of the leaves. "What have you got in there, anyway?" she asked.

"Salad," Ramona said.

"I know that, but what kind?"

"Dandelion, frisee, and some herbs."

"There's nothing poisonous, is there? Or anything that is part of a potion or spell?"

"You're so uptight."

Dan opened the door. Lina's heart stopped, then sailed up to her esophagus and lodged in her throat. He looked adorable. His fine brown hair was a little too short, as if he'd just gotten it cut, which made him look like a little boy. He was wearing a blue button-down shirt that brought out his straight-shooter eyes, and jeans with a cloth belt decorated with Morse Code flags. Or something. All Lina knew was it was supposed to be nautical.

"Two of my favorite writers," Dan said. "Come on in."

Several students and teachers were already there.

Camille Barker, the French teacher, smiled and took Lina's dish from her. "It's wild rice," Lina said.

"Smells good," Camille said. She put the rice on the buffet table and peered into Ramona's bowl. "Salad! Grand." She looked even prettier than usual that evening; her black bob with extra-short bangs was glossy and very French-looking. She wore a white shirt-dress, collar up, belted, full-skirted, fresh and stylish.

"Help yourselves to water, lemonade, or iced tea," Dan said, holding out plastic cups.

"Do they have Jagermeister?" Ramona whispered to Lina. "Because I could really use a shot."

"Why are *you* so nervous?" Lina asked, feeling shaky. "*I'm* the one who's taking a huge chance tonight. Risking severe humiliation and heartbreak. Or arrest. Or worse."

"I'm your accomplice," Ramona said. "And I'm feeling your pain. It's what friends do. In case you didn't know."

Lina fixed herself some iced tea and surveyed the house. She'd been there once before, to deliver a love poem to Dan (God, that was so obvious and stupid, she thought now), but she hadn't gotten past the front hallway. The house was tiny. To the right of the entranceway, the party was centered around the living room/dining room/kitchenette with breakfast bar. To the left, Lina vaguely sensed a bathroom, a hall closet, and a bedroom.

The bedroom door was closed. Off limits. But not for long.

More students and teachers arrived. The principal, John Alvarado, or "Rod," as Dan, and now Lina, secretly called him, greeted everyone with as much warmth as he was capable of summoning. Three English teachers, including Frieda Gantner, the faculty advisor of the *Seer*, clustered around the guacamole and chips. Ramona's friends and fellow *Inchworm* editors, Siobhan Gallagher, Chandra Bledsoe, and Maggie Schwartzman, all dressed like Ramona in copycat black chiffon, black or purple nail polish, and heavy Goth makeup, fluttered around her.

Lina was lining up at the buffet when Walker came in. She smiled at him and nodded, offering him a place with her in line. Instead he turned around and started talking to Kate Bryson. Had he seen Lina? She thought he had. But maybe she was wrong.

She filled her plate and squeezed onto the couch. Ramona plopped down beside her.

"I scoped out the bedroom. Nice big closet in there. Should be a piece of cake," Ramona whispered.

"How did you get in there? The door's closed."

"I just pretended I had to go to the bathroom, then I slipped in. By the way, have you been to the bathroom yet? He's got nose-hair clippers in the medicine cabinet. There's something so cute about that. And an old leftover prescription with some girl's name on it, from like three years ago! Must be an old girlfriend."

"What was her name?"

"Alice Calabresi."

"Alice?" Lina said. "That's my middle name."

"It's a sign," Ramona said. Lina sifted this information through her mind. Could it be a sign of something? Maybe Dan had a thing for the name Alice. It might be a good idea to drop her middle name into a conversation with him if she could.

"Look, your two boyfriends are talking to each other," Ramona said. Walker leaned on the breakfast bar, talking to Dan. What could they be talking about? Walker said something that made Dan laugh.

"He's not my boyfriend," Lina said, and they both knew that she meant Walker.

Camille interrupted Walker and Dan, handing Dan a plate loaded with lasagna and salad. Lina thought she caught Dan doing a little bump against her, hip to hip.

"Did you see that?" she asked Ramona.

"Hip bump at one o'clock. Caught it," Ramona said. "What is up with that?"

"I mean, I knew they were friends but—" Lina said.

"Yeah, I know. Is there more to it? It's hard to tell, since Mademoiselle is such a shameless flirt. Did I tell you

I caught her in the art room one day, draped all over one of the tables, flirting her skinny little butt off with Frank?"

"Really? Why would she bother?" Frank Welling was the art teacher. Thin, weary-faced, long brown mustache. Not nearly as appealing as Dan.

"Maybe she's a compulsive flirt," Ramona said. "Otherwise known as a slut."

"I don't think we know enough about her to say that," Lina said, though she privately thought it might be true.

"Look! He's eating my salad." Ramona sighed and Dan speared a weed with his fork and gnawed on it. "Dan is eating my salad. I hope he likes the powdered Viagra I put in the dressing."

"Ramona!"

"Kidding. Why would I do that?"

"Because you're crazy?"

"Only if you measure me by the rigid norms of society."

"That's the definition of crazy," Lina said.

"Oh, stop being Miss Fussypants."

After dessert Rod made a speech about the importance of writing, self-expression, the free press, and whole language reading programs. It was almost eight o'clock. The party began to break up. People took their dirty casserole dishes and headed for the door. It had been a pleasant enough but fairly dull dinner, as school events usually were.

Guess I'd better make my move, Lina thought as the crowd thinned. She couldn't wait too long or she'd be conspicuous. Her stomach began to twitch and twist, and she regretted eating even a mouthful at dinner. She couldn't believe she was about to do what she was about to do.

She headed for the bathroom, opened the door, and flicked on the light. Then she glanced back. No one was looking. She switched off the bathroom light and reached for the bedroom doorknob. This was it. She was about to enter *his bedroom.*

The door opened easily. She slipped inside and shut the door quickly.

A lamp by the bed was on, and the orange-yellow light of the dwindling day illuminated the room. Lina took a quick look around. The place was a mess. A pigsty. The unmade bed was just a futon on the floor, and there were clothes and magazines and books and papers everywhere. Lina never imagined Dan to be so disorganized.

She spotted the guitar he'd mentioned in his e-mails to Larissa, and the rack of ties, and the hats. Then she heard a noise outside the room and quickly darted to the closet. It was shallow but wide, with accordion doors slightly ajar. Lina pushed the door open and stepped inside.

"Ow!"

Lina jumped. What was that?

"You almost broke my hand!"

Lina looked down. There, huddled in the dark, was Ramona.

"What are you doing here?" Lina whispered.

"Sshh!" Ramona tugged on Lina's hem. "Just get down and shut the door. But not all the way. Leave a crack so we can see."

In her confusion, Lina did as she was told.

"Why are you in here?" she demanded. "I thought we agreed *I* was going to be the one—"

"You would have totally screwed it up," Ramona said. "I'm actually surprised you made it this far. I thought you'd chicken out. And if you did, I'd be here to pick up the reins."

Lina's jaw dropped. How could Ramona be so conniving? And have such a low opinion of her?

"Have you been just pretending to be my friend all this time, so you could get to Dan?" Lina asked.

"No. I like you. We're friends. But as you know, I'll do anything to get to Dan. And I also know you too well. You'll never go through with this. Too many scruples."

"Obviously you don't know me that well, because you thought I'd chicken out, and here I am."

"I still say you'd hide in the closet all night if you had to," Ramona said.

"I'm not going to do anything with you hiding in the closet!" Lina said. "Get out! Quick! Before he comes in!"

"You get out! I was here first."

"But we agreed—and it was my idea."

"No it wasn't. I think it was my idea."

"Look, just go!"

"I'm not going anywhere."

Lina was fuming. Everything was ruined. What would happen when Dan caught the two of them hiding in his closet? They'd look like idiots, or stalkers, or idiotic stalkers.

"You're having second thoughts," Ramona said. "I can feel it."

"You're right," Lina said. "I'm getting out of here. Good luck."

She moved to get out of the closet, but at that moment the bedroom door flew open. Ramona grabbed Lina's hand. They peeked through the cracks in the closet door.

Dan stumbled into the room, pulling Camille behind him. "Ugh. Thank god that's over," he said.

"I know," Camille said. "I thought Rod would never leave. And those Goth girls! Lingering around the kitchen, offering to help clean up . . . I think they have crushes on you."

Lina and Ramona exchanged a glance. Siobhan,

Maggie, and Chandra, up to no good themselves. Luckily, they weren't as clever as Lina and Ramona. Or was it foolish?

"Well, they're all gone now," Dan said, taking Camille in his arms. Lina held her breath. She didn't want to watch, but she couldn't tear her eyes away. They kissed and kissed and kissed until they flopped down on the bed.

Lina's heart stopped. Camille! She knew it! She'd always wondered if there was something between them, and now it seemed clear that there was. Dan and Camille. No wonder "Beau's" e-mails to Larissa had been slacking off lately—he had fallen in love with someone else. The French teacher. Lina squeezed her eyes shut to keep the tears from popping out. She felt like such an idiot.

Ramona yanked on her dress and mimed panic— What were they going to do? They were trapped in a closet, and from the looks of things, they were about to witness two teachers going at it. A terrible experience from which they would never recover. They had to get out some-how—but how? Without looking like spies, weirdos, per-verts . . . you name it.

Lina peeked into the room. The kissing was intensi-fying, accompanied by clothes-tugging. Chance of nudity, 100 percent. They had to work fast. Lina wanted to get out of there before anything too disturbing happened.

Ramona reached into the folds of her dress and

pulled out—eureka!—her cell phone. She pointed at it, nodding, in case Lina didn't get the idea. Lina rolled her eyes and nodded. Ramona scanned through her pro-grammed numbers until she found Dan's. Lina couldn't believe Ramona had Dan's home phone in her cell. Did she ever secretly call him and hang up? Probably. Even Lina hadn't gone that far.

Ramona pressed Dial. Instantly, a phone rang out somewhere in the room. Ramona gave five manic nods, as if to say, See? This will work. *But how?* Lina wondered. *He'll just answer the phone—and then what?*

Dan and Camille broke apart, looking dazed and disheveled. Dan scrambled among the t-shirts and boxer shorts on the floor, feeling around for the phone. It rang again and again. It must be portable, Lina thought, and he can't find it in all the mess.

"Let the machine get it," Camille said, pulling Dan back into bed. After another ring the machine picked up. Lina could hear Dan's recorded voice out in the kitchen. Ramona hung up.

Great. So much for that.

But Ramona didn't give up. Dan and Camille resumed their makeout session. Ramona pressed Redial. The phone rang again.

"Damn it," Dan muttered. He struggled to his feet

and pawed through the junk on his desk, looking for the phone. He couldn't find it. The machine picked up again. Ramona hung up on it.

Dan went back to the bed. Ramona pushed Redial.

"Just ignore it," Camille said, looking frustrated. "Come on, you'll never find it in this mess."

"I can't take that ringing. It's too distracting," Dan said. His hair stuck up around his head, his shirt was untucked and half-unbuttoned.

"If it's important they'll leave a message," Camille said.

"It's not that," Dan said. "It's the noise. If I can't find the phone, I can't turn the ringer off." He stomped barefoot out to the kitchen. Camille got up and slipped into the hallway. Lina saw the bathroom light go on and the door close.

They heard Dan's voice from the kitchen. "Hello?"

Ramona hung up. Lina pushed open the closet door and they scrambled out. Luckily, the bedroom window was open. Lina pulled the screen out, tossed it on the grass below, and dove out the window. Ramona tumbled out behind her, nearly landing on her head.

"Lucky there's only one floor," Ramona whispered as they ran through the shadowy yard, around the house to the street. Lina looked back. No one was following them.

She was pretty sure they hadn't been seen. Still, they didn't stop running until they got to the end of the block, just to be safe.

"That was *this* close to turning into a porno movie right in front of our eyes," Ramona said after she'd caught her breath.

"That was the stupidest thing I've ever done," Lina said quietly.

"Don't beat yourself up. If it had worked it would have been great."

"That's the stupid part. Thinking that plan could ever have worked."

They sat down on a bench at a bus stop. Neither one spoke for several long minutes. Lina was lost in her own thoughts.

Seeing Dan with Camille—a woman his own age, one of his colleagues—struck a nerve in Lina. It was horrible to see him kiss another woman. But it made Lina realize how foolish she'd been, too. She had a crush on her teacher. It wasn't love. It was silly. How could she ever have taken it so seriously? How could she and Ramona have let it go so far?

"You know what?" Lina said at last. "I think it cured me. That nightmare we just narrowly averted cured me."

"What do you mean?"

"I'm over him. You want to keep obsessing, be my guest. But I think I'll bow out before I do something *really* stupid."

"Have no fear," Ramona said. "New reasons to do something stupid are plentiful. All we have to do is stumble over one."

"Until then," Lina said, "no more nutty Dan plans. I'm going straight."

Just saying the words—and knowing she meant them, really meant them this time—made her feel better.

16 Blind Item

To:	mad4u
From:	your daily horoscope

HERE IS TODAY'S HOROSCOPE: VIRGO: There's no law against plotting and scheming . . . unless you count karma.

Stupid Rod," Mads muttered as she slammed her locker shut and trudged down the empty hallway. It was late on Wednesday afternoon, and almost everybody had left school for the day. At lunchtime, Principal Alvarado had asked Mads to come talk to him in his office after school. Mads was shaky and nervous for the rest of the afternoon. She couldn't eat. What could the principal want to talk to her about? Had she done something wrong? Was she in trouble? She racked her brain trying to think of what it could be. That C she got on her Geometry quiz? Something she wrote on the Web site?

By the time the day ended and she wound up at his office, she was pale and shaking. "If you don't hear from me by nine tonight, tell my parents to call the cops," she said to Lina before she went in. "And send dogs. Those sniffing kind."

Lina waved this away. "Rod won't hurt you. You'll be fine. But IM me as soon as you get home. I'm dying to know what you did."

The principal smiled at her as she opened the door and waved her to a seat. "Thanks for coming, Madison," he said. "Do you have a few minutes?"

"Well—" It depended what for, obviously. But what was she going to say, "No"?

"I just wanted to talk to you about your extracurricular activities."

Oh god. Did he mean that beer she'd had at Nick Henin's party? Did he somehow hear about her crazed quest to lose her virginity?

"Your mother's play. I'm a big theater buff. What's it about?"

Oh, that. He kept Mads in his office for almost an hour discussing *Touched: The Story of a Sensitive Girl,* how the costumes and sets would be handled, who the director was, and if Mads thought he was any good. It turned out Rod was working on a play himself (tentative title: *Learning Curve, a Principal's Private Struggle*), and he was hoping to have it produced.

He finally let her go when she pretended to look at the watch she wasn't really wearing and said her mother was expecting her at rehearsal soon. Suddenly she was starving. She hadn't eaten lunch—for this? All that terror for nothing.

Mads left the school building, not really thinking about where she was going. She found her feet moving in the direction of the swim center. Funny, because Sean was on the swim team and would probably be finishing practice soon. What a coincidence.

Sean burst out of the swim center, hair wet and smelling of chlorine, just as she was passing by. Finally a little luck.

Now was her chance. She'd been waiting for a moment alone with him all week, and this was perfect. Mads was going to do it. She was going to tell him. About Jane. And wait for him to fall into her arms.

Soon she would be on the escalator to ecstasy.

"Sean!" she called, waving to him. He stopped on the swim center steps. She ran over to him.

"Hey, kid, whatup?" Sean said.

This was it. Did she have the guts to do it? You bet she did.

"I have something important to tell you," Mads began.

"Hey, whatever happened to that article you were supposed to be doing about me. For the *Seer*? Did that ever come out?"

Uh-oh. Mads had gotten Lina to pretend to interview Sean for the paper so Mads could take a picture of him in his bathing suit. But it was just a scam. There was no article. And Mads didn't expect Sean to remember it.

"Um, Lina's still working on it," Mads lied. "She's a terrible procrastinator. I don't know how she ever gets an article published."

"Maybe she's got A.D.D.," Sean said. "I used to be that way, until I started swimming. If I don't swim, I get *spacy*."

"I'll mention that to her."

"Or you can take the drugs," Sean said. "But Ritalin made me sleepy."

"Huh." Mads was beginning to wish he'd never brought this up. "Anyway, um, this is something I think you'll be very interested to know." She paused, trying to come up with the most effective way to say it. A way that wouldn't make her look like a gossip, but like someone who had his best interests at heart. "You know that play I'm in, with Jane?"

"Oh, yeah. The *Touched* thing. Jane says it totally blows."

Mads was caught short by this. It was one thing for *her* to say that her mother's play sucked. And another thing for Jane to say it to Mads in the spirit of actorly cama- raderie. But the thought of Jane going home from rehearsal and telling *Sean* that Mads' mother's play was bad . . . that was different. That was crossing a line. Somehow.

Put that out of your mind, Mads told herself. *You have a mission to accomplish*. And if she accomplished it, it would get Jane back for the mean comment.

"Speaking of Jane—" Mads began, but at that moment a gang of boys trooped back from the lacrosse field, dangling their helmets from their sticks.

"Sean!" one of them called, and soon Sean and Mads were surrounded by five sweaty lacrosse players. "Dude, when are you going to quit splashing in the pool like a sissy and play a real sport?"

"Sissy?" Sean poked the guy's shoulder pads. "Look at you, helmet, pads. . . . You can't step on the field until your mommy says it's safe to play."

The guys all laughed.

"It's better than wearing a thong," another guy said.

Sean snatched his wet Speedo out of his backpack and aimed it at the guy like a slingshot. "Watch it or you'll get it right in the face," he joked.

"Hey, don't wave that thing at me." The boys backed up, hands in the air, laughing. Then they marched toward the gym locker room. Sean twirled the bathing suit around his finger like a six-shooter and dropped it in his pack.

"All right, kid, I gotta go," he said, starting to walk away.

"Wait!" Why was it so hard to talk to him? He couldn't seem to keep his mind on one thing. "This won't take long. I saw something at rehearsal that—"

The swim center doors burst open and three girls, green-haired from too much chlorine, tripped down the steps, chattering and laughing. Sean turned his head toward them. Mads tried to ignore them. She should have known better.

"Hey, Sean." The girls slowed their pace, walking past Sean and Mads as if on display.

Sean grinned. "Hey, girls. Good practice?"

"Excellent practice," one of the girls said. "Shaved two-tenths of a second off my hundred-meter freestyle."

"All right," Sean said. "Coach says I need a little work on my breaststroke. Maybe one of you could tutor me?"

The girls giggled. Mads rolled her eyes at his lame joke. How could he be wasting his time flirting with these floozies when his relationship with Jane was in deep trouble? Maybe this was why Jane was restless. Mads was beginning to sympathize with her.

"Sean, you're terrible." The girls waved coquettishly as they ambled away. Mads could tell they were all very aware of how they were walking, in case Sean was watching them. And he was.

When they'd rounded the corner out of sight Sean said, "Okay, time to head home—"

"Sean, stop." Mads grabbed him by the wrist, surprised at her own boldness. He must have been surprised, too, because she'd finally gotten his attention. "Listen to me. At rehearsal the other day I—I saw Jane, backstage, and she was *kissing*—"

"Jane!" Sean's face lit up. Mads turned and saw Jane walking toward them.

"There you are," she said.

"See ya, kid," Sean said. He yanked his wrist out of Mads' grip and walked away from her. Right in the middle of a sentence. Even after she had said the word "kissing." Didn't that interest him? "I saw Jane, and she was kissing . . ." Who? Another boy? Mads' mother? An orangutan? Didn't he want to know? Had he heard a word she'd said? Did he ever listen to her?

He grabbed Jane, kissed her, and said, "Way to surprise me."

"I was driving by and I thought I'd give you a ride, if

you were still here," Jane said. She waved at Mads. "Hi, Madison! See you at rehearsal later!"

The two of them walked off arm in arm. Mads stood alone on the path between the swim center and the main school building, crushed.

What was it with Sean? Why did he always act as if she were invisible?

She fumed about Sean and Jane all the way home. Later that night, in her room, she came to a decision.

That's it, she thought. Sean didn't want to listen to her? She'd make him pay attention. And she knew the perfect way.

El Diario

Today's blind items: What bookish junior is head-over-heels in love for the very first time with a dashing college student?

What sophomore girl went totally yellular in the lunch room yesterday, screaming at her father so loud on her cell that the whole room could hear? Think of seasons, back to school, leaves falling, certain blog that's atomically popular . . .

I saved the best for last. What leggy blonde is cheating on her sexy swimmer boyfriend? Here's a clue.

The answer rhymes with pain.

17 Good-bye, Dan.
Hello, Donald Death.

To:	linaonme
From:	your daily horoscope

HERE IS TODAY'S HOROSCOPE: CANCER: Welcome back to
Planet Earth. It sucks, doesn't it?

Dear Larissa,

*How are you? Hope things are great in India. I'm writing
to explain why I haven't been e-mailing you so often lately—
and will probably be in touch even less in the future. I've kind of
fallen for someone. Someone I work with. We have to keep it quiet
for now, until the end of the year. But since I'm leaving anyway,
we're not too worried about getting caught.*

*I know you might be surprised, but after all, you and I
have never met. We've never even spoken to each other. Though I*

have to say I fell for you, too, in a way. I wish things could have worked out between us. I was upset when you told me you were moving to India. It's so far away. But much as I treasure your friendship, I need a real live person to be with, in the flesh. I'm sure you understand. I've often had the feeling that you were involved with someone—or more than one person—during our correspondence. Maybe that's why you were a little reluctant to meet.

I'd still like to hear from you once in a while. Let me know when your first screenplay is produced! I'll go see the movie and be your biggest fan.

Love,

Beauregard

Lina got up from her computer, sighed, and flopped down on the bed. This kiss-off e-mail was the final straw. It was over. Really over.

In a way it was a relief. All the lying, the plotting, the scheming, the daydreaming—it took a lot of energy. And what did she ever get out of it? Nothing, really. But she felt sad, almost as if she'd lost a real boyfriend. There was a hole in her life now. Dan was gone. Lina wasn't quite sure what to do with herself.

She printed out the e-mail, stuffed it in her bag, and rode her bike to Ramona's house. Ramona had invited her over for a Cleansing Ceremony. She had a shrine in her room called the Museum of Dan, filled with pictures of him, papers he'd graded, his used coffee cups, even a pizza crust he once threw away. Ramona and her friends used to perform love ceremonies at the shrine, hoping to make Dan fall for them. Proof, Lina thought, that all that stuff was crap.

Still, a Cleansing Ceremony seemed like a good idea, for mental health. Lina found Ramona in her room, gathering all the museum exhibits in a pile.

"Now that I look at the stuff, I realize it's nothing but trash," Ramona said, dumping it in a metal waste basket. "It's time to get rid of it. It was attracting ants."

Lina showed her Dan's final e-mail. Ramona read it and tossed it onto the pile in the basket. Then she took both of Lina's hands. "Close your eyes," Ramona said.

Ramona closed her eyes.

"Daniel Shulman, we thank you for all you have given us," Ramona said. "But now it is time to move on. You will always be our first love. May you find happiness with that pseudo-French twit."

Lina opened one eye, and caught Ramona with both eyes open. She glared at Lina, who quickly shut hers again.

Ramona shook their hands over the pile three

times. "Say it with me, Lina: Good-bye, good luck, good riddance."

"Good-bye, good luck, good riddance," Lina said.

"Okay. You can open your eyes."

Lina opened her eyes. Ramona sprinkled some kind of pink powder on the trash. Then she lit a match and set it on fire. The trash can was tall enough to contain the small flames. It flared up for a minute, then slowly died down until it was out.

Ramona poked through the ashes. "The pizza crust didn't really burn," she said. "But close enough. It's over. No more Dan. He's out of our lives."

"Right." Lina wasn't sure what to say or do next. She and Ramona were very different people; their bond had been their shared love for Dan. Would they grow apart now? Lina hoped not. She had come to rely on Ramona for a certain type of blunt kindness. "What do we do now?"

"Well, I'm not the kind of girl who can go shrine-free for very long," Ramona said. She pulled out a huge poster of a Goth-metal rock star named Donald Death. His face was powdered white, with pointed black brows, heavy eyeliner, red lipstick, and those weird contact lenses that make you look like an alien. In one eye, at least; the other was hidden by a black patch.

"My next obsession: Deathzilla," Ramona said. Deathzilla was the name of Donald Death's band. She tacked the poster up on the oriental screen that had once held shavings from Dan's pencil sharpener. "Join me?"

Lina shuddered at the leer on Donald's face. "A worthy idol. But not my type."

Lina couldn't go home yet. She still felt that emptiness, and there was no way a quiet night with Ken and Sylvia in their spare, boxy house would fill it. No, this was a job for Mads and Holly.

She rode her bike straight to Mads' house. "Let's bake some cookies," Mads said, leading Lina to the funky farm-house-style kitchen. Captain Meow-Meow, Mads' Siamese cat, lounged on the wooden table. "The kitchen's off limits!" she shouted to the household in general.

"No fair!" Audrey yelled back.

"Deal with it," Mads said. She sat Lina at the table and started bringing out bowls for mixing and butter for softening.

"I called Holly, but she was busy," Mads reported. "Guess why?"

"Britta crisis?" Lina asked.

Mads nodded. "She didn't say what it was."

"Britta's life is so dramatic, like an opera," Lina said.

"Regular or soap?" Mads said.

"Either one," Lina said. "But I was thinking of regular opera. Big emotions, lots of passion. Even when something bad happens, I bet she never feels empty."

Mads gave her a funny look. "That's true. Anyway, Holly said she'd try to get here later." Mads opened a bag of chocolate chips and started nibbling on them. "You look sad."

"I know. It's just . . . Dan. Ramona has already moved on. But I feel stuck. I don't know what's wrong with me."

"Nothing's wrong with you," Mads said. "Ramona's the weirdo. You just feel things more deeply."

"What about you? Did you tell Sean about Jane yet?"

"He won't listen to me." She bit the tiny point off the top of a chip. "Why won't he listen to me, Lina? He makes me feel invisible. Or worse, beneath visibility. Like an ant on the sidewalk—you could see it if you looked, but you don't bother, so you step on it without realizing what you're doing."

"It's not you, Mads," Lina said. "He likes you, in his own way. He just doesn't see much beyond himself."

"You make him sound like a jerk."

Lina decided it was best not to say anything.

"I never understood why you liked Dan, either," Mads said. She grinned and handed Lina a spoon and a bowl with a stick of butter in it. "Start mashing."

Smushing and stirring and playing with dough cheered them both up, and soon the smell of baking cookies drew Audrey to the kitchen.

"Out," Mads said.

"Can't I have a cookie?" Audrey asked.

"When they're ready," Mads said. "We'll let you know. We'll get back to you. Out."

Audrey sat down at the table. "See how she listens to me?" Mads said. "Nobody listens to me."

"I think you're wrong about Jane and Damien," Audrey said to Mads.

"How do you know about that?" Mads asked.

"I read it on your blog. *El Diarrhea*."

"How could I be wrong?" Mads said. "Did you see them making out in the back of the theater today?"

"Yeah, but think about it," Audrey said. "Damien plays Jane's boyfriend. They're trying to *live* their roles. It's the Method."

Mads rolled her eyes. "Damien plays my boyfriend, too, and you don't see him sticking his tongue down my throat every five minutes."

"That's because you're so hopeless even the Method can't save you," Audrey said.

"Sean's sure to figure it out now," Lina said. "Since you

practically spelled it out for him on the blog."

"If he reads it," Mads said. "I just wish he could see that tall and blond and pretty and super-cool aren't everything. Short and dark-haired can be fun, too."

"Why don't you just give it up?" Audrey said.

Mads tilted Audrey's chair forward and dumped her on the floor. "Leave. And just for that, you get no cookies."

Audrey tossed her ponytail. "You haven't seen the last of Audrey Markowitz. I'll be back."

Lina laughed. "Come on. You have to admit she's cute."

"Only someone lucky enough to have zero siblings would say that," Mads said.

While they waited for the cookies to bake, Lina noticed a different kind of emptiness in the room. Not the loss of Dan. Something else.

"Doesn't it feel weird to be doing stuff without Holly all the time?" she said to Mads.

"Yeah," Mads said. "Do you think she likes Britta more than she likes us?"

"That's impossible," Lina said.

"It kind of feels that way," Mads said.

"To me it feels more like she's taking us for granted," Lina said. "You know how Holly loves matchmaking. And Britta's got this storybook love thing going on, and Holly's all caught up in it—"

"It *is* amazing," Mads said.

"It is, right?" Lina said. "So Holly doesn't have much time for us now."

"I understand," Mads said. "But still, I don't like being taken for granted."

"Me, neither," Lina said.

18 Britta Takes the Plunge

To:	hollygolitely
From:	your daily horoscope

HERE IS TODAY'S HOROSCOPE: CAPRICORN: You will face a test today, and this time you won't be able to cheat by scribbling the answers on your hand.

Holly sat in the front seat of her VW and watched Britta drive away. Britta was a mess. She kept talking about how she wished she could move to England with Ed. How horrible her life would be if she had to stay here without him. All the wonderful things he said to her . . . All the wonderful things he did for her. . . .

Holly was exhausted. They'd talked so long the waitress at Vineland had to kick them out so she could close up. It was almost midnight.

Holly was supposed to stop by Mads' house, but it was too late now. She started the car and let the engine idle while she called Mads on her cell phone.

"Where are you?" Mads asked. "Lina's here, but she has to go home in a minute."

"I know, I'm sorry," Holly said. "I couldn't get away. But I'll make it up to you. What if all three of us go to the movies tomorrow night to see *Kiss Me, Stinky?*"

"Um, *Kiss Me, Stinky?*" Mads said. Then she paused. Holly thought she heard Mads murmur something to someone in the room with her. Probably Lina.

"Can we see something else?" Mads said. "How about *Rocket to Russia?*"

"What? No," Holly said. "We agreed. We all want to see *Kiss Me, Stinky* together. Right?"

Another pause. What was going on?

"Mads?"

"Holly, Lina and I already saw it," Mads said.

Holly thought she must have heard wrong. "What?"

"We already saw it."

"Without me? But we were going to see it together! We agreed!" Holly felt stung.

"I know," Mads said. "We called you but you were

with Britta. We needed cheering up that night and it was the perfect thing—"

Holly almost felt like crying. "I can't believe you went without me."

"I'm sorry," Mads said. "But you're never free. You're always doing something with Britta."

"You don't understand," Holly said. "Britta is in a terrible situation. She really needs me!"

"We need you, too," Mads said.

Holly felt a pang of guilt. She didn't know what to say to that. Had she been neglecting her best friends?

"Lina has to get going," Mads said. "We'll talk to you tomorrow."

She hung up. Holly shifted the car into drive and headed for home through the dark, quiet streets of Carlton Bay. She tried to be angry with them—*How could they have gone without me?* But it didn't last. She knew Mads and Lina were right. She'd been neglecting them. And Rob, too. She'd dropped everything to live Britta's big love story with her. It was just that Holly had never been through anything like that, never had anything like that herself. Mads and Lina had their dramatic crushes, their huge ups and downs that depended on what Dan or Sean had said or done that moment. But Britta's love was real.

Holly parked in the driveway and walked slowly

along the landscaped path to the house. She opened the door and found Jen waiting for her. "Thank god you're home!" Jen said. "Britta's not with you?"

"No," Holly said. "We went to Vineland, and then she went home."

"No, she didn't," Jen said. "Peggy Fowler just called to talk to Britta. Britta told her she was spending the night here."

"She did?" Uh-oh. Why didn't Britta warn her? Should she make up a lie to cover for her?

"Peggy wants you to call her right away," Jen said.

Oh, no, Holly thought, crossing the room to the kitchen phone. She had a bad feeling about this.

"Britta's not with you?" Peggy Fowler cried. "Where could she be?"

"Well, I'm not sure—" Holly said.

"Holly, we're frantic," Peggy Fowler said. "She told us she was spending the night with you! She lied to us!" She choked back a sob. "She's been acting so strangely lately. Please, Holly. It's after midnight and we have no idea where she could be. Do you know anything? Did she say anything to you?"

Oh my god, Holly thought as the truth dawned on her. *She's done it! She ran away to marry Ed!* Holly couldn't help admiring Britta. She wasn't all talk—she was willing to do whatever it took to be with the guy she loved. But the admiration faded to worry, then fear, then panic. Britta had eloped! This was for real. No turning back.

"Holly, we're desperate," Peggy said. "We're so worried about her! She spends so much time with you. You must have some idea where she could be."

Holly did have an idea. *But I promised Britta I wouldn't tell,* Holly thought, stalling for time. *How can I betray her?*

Peggy started crying. "She's in some kind of trouble, I just know it. Please, Holly. Help me."

The desperation in Peggy's voice scared Holly. Peggy was terrified. Her daughter had disappeared. Holly knew Britta was probably not in any physical danger. But she was taking a huge step. It would have major consequences, and Holly knew, from talking to her, that Britta hadn't really thought it through. She didn't know what she was getting into. She was blinded by love.

She'd promised not to tell the Fowlers that Britta planned to get married. But they were so worried. As far as they knew, Britta could be dead. Holly couldn't let them think that when it wasn't true. It was too mean.

Holly had no choice. She had to tell the Fowlers what was going on.

She took a deep breath. "I think I know where you can find her," Holly said. "There's an empty house near the beach, on Sandhill Road. With a 'For Sale' sign out front. She and Ed go there. It's their secret hideaway."

"Why? Why would she be there at this hour?" Peggy asked.

Holly swallowed. "Well, they might be planning to elope."

"What?" Peggy screamed. "She's going to marry that boy?"

"I could be wrong—" Holly said, but she knew she wasn't.

"Gordon, get the car!" Peggy yelled. She hung up on Holly without saying good-bye.

"Britta Fowler?" Jen gave a throaty chuckle. "Britta Fowler wants to elope? With a boy?"

"It's not funny, Jen," Holly said.

"Come on, honey," Jen said. "Miss Future Harvard? The girl who studied all the time and never had a date? You have to admit—"

"It's not funny to her," Holly said. "She's serious about it."

"She's serious about everything," Jen said. "Anyway, honey, I'm glad you told the Fowlers. You did the right thing. She must be out of her mind."

A few minutes later, Curt came home, having been out late entertaining clients. Or something. The three of them sat at the kitchen table drinking decaf and waiting for news of Britta. Holly started to get nervous. What if she was wrong? What if Britta hadn't eloped? What if something terrible—something truly terrible—had happened to her instead?

After a couple hours of waiting, the phone finally rang. Holly answered it.

"We found her, Holly," Peggy said. "Right where you said she would be. They were going to get married in the morning."

"Is she okay?"

"We've got her home safe now. Thank you for your help, Holly. She's very upset."

Holly felt all mixed up—relieved and guilty at the same time. She was glad Britta was okay. But Holly had betrayed her trust. And she never thought she'd do that to a friend.

"Someday Britta will thank us," Peggy said. "You did the right thing, Holly."

I hope so, Holly thought. *I really do.*

19 The Pain in Rain

"Mads, you scooped me," Autumn Nelson said in the hallway at school. "I had no idea Rain was cheating on Caleb!"

"What?" Mads glanced at Stephen, who was heading to lunch with her, to see if this made any more sense to him than it did to her. He shrugged and shook his head.

"Going to lunch?" Autumn asked. "Let's walk and talk." She marched alongside Mads and Stephen as they walked through the hall. "What I want to know is, how did you catch her? And who is the other guy?"

"Um—" Mads had been waiting all morning for the fallout from her blind gossip item about Sean and Jane to bear fruit. But Jane didn't go to RSAGE—she was in college—and Mads hadn't seen Sean around anywhere. Autumn seemed to be talking about something that happened in a parallel universe. A girl cheating on her boyfriend, yes. But who were Caleb and Rain?

"Everybody's talking about it," Autumn said. "We're just waiting for the two of them to implode. So tell me, who is it? Is it Mo?"

"Um, Autumn? What are you talking about?" Mads asked. They reached the lunchroom and hesitated at the threshold. Autumn and Mads didn't usually sit together, and the rigid code of the lunchroom was rarely breached. Mads didn't want to sit with her, anyway. She wanted to have a nice quiet lunch with Stephen.

Autumn waved to her friends across the room, as if to say "Be there in a minute." "Hello?" she said to Mads. "You wrote it? On your blog? El Diarrhea?"

Mads flinched. "Funny, that's what my sister calls it, too."

"You said a swimmer's girlfriend was cheating on him and she's blond and her name rhymes with 'pain,'" Autumn said. "Who else could it be?"

Mads hadn't thought of that. Now that Autumn mentioned it, there was a swimmer named Caleb on the team, and there was a blond girl in the senior class named Rain Something-or-other. But Mads had no idea they were going out. And she'd also said the swimmer's girlfriend was leggy, and Mads wouldn't exactly call Rain leggy. Unless leggy could describe short, powerful soccer-type legs, which was what Rain had.

While Mads thought all this through, Stephen said, "I'll go save us a spot at the table," and went with his bag lunch to their usual place.

"Autumn, I hardly know them," Mads said. "Caleb and Rain, I mean. I—"

"Autumn!" Rebecca Hulse screeched across the lunch-room. "Get over here!"

Autumn sighed. "She's such a bitch. All right, we'll talk later." She hurried over to her table. Mads joined Stephen at theirs.

"This is about that blind item on your blog, isn't it," Stephen said.

"You read it?" Mads had kind of hoped he'd skip that part.

"Of course," Stephen said. "I check the Dating Game every day for new entries. It's my guide to the inner work-ings of your mind."

"Really?" Mads was both flattered and horrified. El

Diario did reflect some of the inner workings of her mind—the silliest. "I wouldn't take that stuff too seriously, you know. I mean, I'm writing for an audience. It's not a true reflection of my personality—"

"Quit backtracking," Stephen said. "It's cute. But I don't really get it. Why are you writing gossip about Caleb and Rain? I've never heard you mention them before."

"It's not about Caleb and Rain," Mads said. She tried to show her best, most noble and intelligent face to Stephen whenever possible, but she was beginning to think it was too late for that now. And she didn't want him to suspect that she still had a crush on Sean, though sometimes she had a feeling that he suspected anyway.

"It's about Sean and Jane," Mads said. "I've seen Jane kissing this guy in the play, Damien, more than once. I thought Sean should know."

"Why?" Stephen asked.

"Well, wouldn't you want to know if I was kissing some other boy?"

"I don't know," Stephen said. "Maybe. It depends why you're kissing him, how serious it is, and if it's worth getting upset over. Because I would get upset. But what if you just kissed him a few times and I never found out about it and it never affected us? Then I'd be getting upset over nothing."

"I don't think this is nothing, though," Mads said. "I think this is something."

"Maybe. But you don't know exactly what kind of something."

"I still think Sean has a right to know," Mads said. "She's deceiving him. If you were cheating on me and Holly knew about it, I'd kill her if she didn't tell me."

"I guess everybody has different feelings about it," Stephen said. He glanced at Mads' lunch, which she had unpacked but not yet touched. "Are you going to eat that cookie?"

Mads put her hand over the cookie protectively. "Yes," she said. "But I brought another one for you." She reached into her bag and brought out an oatmeal cookie wrapped in foil with a heart drawn on it in red marker.

"Hey, thanks." Stephen took the cookie. "That's sweet of you."

"It's not from me. It's from M.C.," Mads said. Her mother loved Stephen. "But I would have done the same thing if she hadn't thought of it first."

There was a crash in the cafeteria food line. Rain dropped her tray and ran into the lunchroom, shrieking, followed by a red-faced, bellowing Caleb. "Just tell me his name!" Caleb roared.

"Caleb, I swear it's not true!" Rain cried. He cornered

her against the far bank of windows. The lunchroom fell silent.

Caleb threw a slice of pizza against the wall—*splat!*—where it stuck for a moment before sliding down in a stream of grease. "You're lying! I always knew there was something weird going on. All those nights you said you were taking tae kwon do—"

"But I *was* taking tae kwon do," Rain said. "And I'll prove it!" She reared back and gave Caleb a mighty kick in the chest—"Hee-ya!" Caleb, big as he was, flew backward and landed on his butt. The room burst into laughter and cheers.

Caleb got to his feet. "I'm going to find out who it is, and I'm going to rip his face off!"

"You do that!" Rain shouted. "Look all over school for the guy I'm supposedly cheating with. That ought to keep you busy while I find a real guy who's not paranoid!"

Caleb stormed out of the room. Rain scanned the tables until her eyes settled on Mads. Mads swallowed. Uh-oh.

"Madison Markowitz?" Rain asked, marching to her table.

Mads tried to smile. "Um, you can call me Mads."

"I'll call you whatever I damn well please," Rain said. "Why did you print that gossip about me? Why would you want to make up lies about me? I don't even know you!"

"It wasn't supposed to be about you, see—"

"You're trying to get Caleb for yourself, is that it?" Rain said. "That's it, isn't it? You're after Caleb. You're trying to break us up!"

"No, see, I never even really noticed him before—"

"Who's this guy?" Rain asked, jerking her thumb at Stephen.

"Hello, I'm the boyfriend," Stephen said. "At least, until Caleb replaces me."

"Stephen!" Mads punched his arm.

"I knew it," Rain said. She stuck her face up close to Mads'. "Listen to me, Madison Markowitz. You're going to be sorry you wrote lies about Rain Rickenbacker, you lying liar. If I see another word about me on that stupid Web site of yours, I'm going to break your fingers. You won't be able to write a word without a voice recognition system!"

"I've heard those can be very frustrating," Stephen said. "They get everything wrong—"

Mads still wanted to explain, if only Rain would listen to her. "See, you still don't get it. It wasn't *about* you, it was about—"

"I'm warning you—your fingers will never touch a

keyboard again. Got me?"

She stormed across the room and burst through the swinging doors. Everyone stared at Mads.

"It was all a—a big mistake," Mads said. "Really. I mean, she could be cheating on him for all I know, but . . . " Mads let her words fade out. It was no use.

Sean walked out of the cafeteria line, tray in hand, and stepped over the puddle of spilt food and broken dishes that Rain had left. He looked up, shook his shaggy blond hair, and said, "What happened? Did I miss something?"

Mads rubbed her head. She was getting a headache.

"Maybe that blind item thing isn't the best way to pass on information," Stephen said. "I mean, you know, as far as accuracy goes."

"You're probably right," Mads admitted. She thought she'd learned to think these things through before she acted on them. Guess not.

20 Rapunzel

HERE IS TODAY'S HOROSCOPE: CAPRICORN: Great news: Your trip to the lower depths won't use up any frequent flier miles.

"Holly, my parents are the forces of evil," Britta wailed. "They're the Taliban. They're Orcs. They're Lord and Lady Voldemort!" She buried her head in her green pillow and sobbed.

"They can't be that bad." Holly sat beside her on the bed, trying to comfort her. Britta had been a mess ever since the Fowlers had dragged her, kicking and screaming, from the beach house. "They're only trying to do what's best for you."

"Ed said that we should have left for Las Vegas right away," Britta said. "But I wanted to spend one last night in our little house. I should have listened to him. We would have been long gone . . . If only I had listened to Ed!"

The Fowlers had found them with their bags packed, ready to leave in the morning. Holly couldn't believe that Britta, this seventeen-year-old girl sitting right in front of her, had come so close to getting married. She felt as if she had just woken up from a gauzy, romantic dream. But Britta was still trapped in the dream.

"They won't let me see Ed at all—ever!" Britta cried. "They make me tell them where I am every second of the day. I have to go straight to school and come straight home and not stop anywhere for a minute. They actually wanted to put a tracking device on me! I'm under house arrest."

Holly wasn't sure what to say. She could understand Britta's frustration, but she saw the Fowlers' side of things, too. After all, Britta did disobey them, lie to them, and run away with a guy she'd known only for a couple of weeks. Even Holly's parents would get upset about that.

Holly crossed the room for a box of Kleenex. It was the greenest room Holly had ever seen. Forest green everything: curtains, walls, bedspread, chairs. *How can she live like this?* Holly wondered. It was like a claustrophobic elves' den. *Even if green were your favorite color,* Holly thought, *you could liven it up with a little white or something.*

Britta sat up and yanked three tissues out of the box. "The part I don't get," she said through her stuffy nose, "is how they knew where to find us."

Holly froze.

"What did they do?" Britta wondered aloud. "Listen in on my phone calls? Have me followed? Read my e-mail? We planned almost everything by e-mail. Do you think they actually found a way to steal my password and read my e-mail?"

Holly felt sick. The Fowlers hadn't told Britta how they found her. She didn't know that Holly had betrayed her trust. And now it was Holly she turned to for comfort, to confide in even further. But what should Holly do? She'd never meant to hurt Britta, only help her. If she confessed to Britta, Britta would only get more upset, feel more alone. Britta needed a friend. Holly decided to be the best friend to her she could.

She gave a stiff shrug. "Who knows how they did it? It doesn't really matter, does it?"

"I don't want them to find out anything else about me, that's all. Maybe we should make up a secret language, a code for all our e-mails, IMs, and phone calls. Something my parents could never decipher . . . "

"Okay," Holly said, though she knew this was completely unnecessary. "Pig Latin?"

"They'd figure that out in a second." Britta thought for a few minutes, then said, "I'll work on it. In the meantime, pass on any important information to me in person only. Unless . . ." She suddenly jumped to her feet and started looking around the room, feeling under the chair and behind the dresser for suspicious lumps. "What if my room is bugged?"

"Britta, calm down," Holly said. "Even *your* parents wouldn't go that far."

"You don't know them." Satisfied after a brief scan, she sat on the bed and dissolved into tears again. "I just miss him so much. . . . "

Holly wished she could turn green and fade into the background. *Maybe I made a terrible mistake,* she thought. *Why does everything I do seem to backfire lately? Rob is annoyed because I've been neglecting him, and Lina and Mads feel neglected, too, and Britta would hate me if she knew the truth. . . . I did the right thing, didn't I?*

By the time Holly left Britta's house, she felt so guilty and low that she knew she couldn't go straight home. She longed to see Lina and Mads. She had no one else to turn to. She knew they were annoyed with her, but they wouldn't shut her out.

She called them on her cell and asked them to meet her at Vineland.

"I'm sorry I haven't been around much lately," Holly said. She and Lina and Mads settled down together on the sofa at Vineland, three hot chocolates lined up on the coffee table in front of them.

"We just missed you," Lina said. "But we know how intense things were with Britta."

"You don't even know how intense," Holly said. "Last night Britta tried to elope with Ed."

Mads gasped. "She was going to marry him?"

"He's going back to England next week, and she wants to be with him. She doesn't care about college or anything anymore."

"What happened?" Lina asked.

Holly hesitated. She wanted to confess what she'd done. Maybe they'd tell her it wasn't so bad. But she was afraid they wouldn't trust her if they knew she'd told on Britta. They might worry that their secrets weren't safe with her.

Holly's silence scared Mads. "Oh my god," she said. "Was there an accident?"

"No, nothing like that," Holly said. She plunged in. "What happened was . . . her mother called looking for her and she was so upset, and I had a feeling I knew where Britta was . . . so I told her mother they were going to elope. And that they were probably at the cottage."

"The beautiful secret beach house?" Mads said.

Holly nodded. "I feel so terrible. Britta made me promise not to tell her parents about it. But I was afraid! And her parents were freaking—"

"Does Britta know you told?" Lina asked.

"No," Holly said. "She doesn't know how they found her. She thinks they've been spying on her or reading her e-mail. If she found out it was me—I think she'd hate me forever."

A silence settled over the couch. Holly glanced at Mads and Lina. What were they thinking? Were they afraid to trust her now?

"Are we still going to Stanford next weekend?" Lina asked.

"Sure, if you want to," Holly said.

"I was going to smack you if you said no," Mads said. "After what I went through to get permission to go."

"What if we brought Britta with us?" Lina said. "It might cheer her up and help her forget about Ed, at least a little."

"And if she has fun, she might be glad she's going to college instead of getting married," Mads added.

"You're not mad at me?" Holly asked. "Or afraid I'll call up your parents and tell them all your secrets?"

"You'd never do that," Lina said. "We've got too much dirt on you."

Holly laughed and felt better. Lina and Mads were the best. "All right," she said. "I'll ask Britta. But it will be a miracle if her parents let her go."

"Woo hoo!" Mads raised her mug. Holly and Lina clinked glasses with her. "The crazy college weekend is a go!"

21 The Crazy College Weekend

To:	hollygolitely
From:	your daily horoscope

HERE IS TODAY'S HOROSCOPE: CAPRICORN: That little twinge you feel, just under your skull? Skip the CAT scan—it's not a brain tumor. It's your conscience.

T hat's Memorial Church," Holly said. Holly's yellow VW Beetle chugged down Palm Drive, the long, straight, tree-lined road that led from the town of Palo Alto to the Stanford University campus. It ended in a beautiful white chapel topped with a dome. "And that's the Main Quad."

Holly had been to Stanford a few times before, the last time being when she and her parents dropped Piper off during Freshman Week back in August.

"It's so beautiful," Mads said as they drove through the campus. "Imagine living here, in a wonderful place like this, with lots of friends and no parents? It's paradise!"

"Only if you're with someone you love," Britta said. That silenced the car for few minutes. For the whole ride—which lasted about an hour and a half—every sentence out of Britta's mouth was a downer. Holly was starting to wish she'd just zip it. She could ruin the whole weekend.

Britta had been reluctant to go when Holly first mentioned it—Ed was leaving on Monday. What if she found a way to see him over the weekend? Since her confinement he'd been secretly texting her in code, begging her to sneak out and see him. But she could never get away.

Holly pointed out that Britta hadn't managed to get past her parents yet and probably never would, so she might as well come away and have a good time. The Fowlers liked the idea of keeping Britta away from Ed and getting her excited about college again. And they trusted Holly, since she'd been honest with them and helped them find Britta when she ran away. To Holly's surprise, they let Britta go. "Think of it as a 'Get out of Jail Free' card," Holly told Britta.

Holly pulled up at Sterling Quad and the girls piled

out. Piper's head popped out of a second-story window. "Welcome to Party Central!"

It was late Friday afternoon, and students buzzed around the quad, setting up for a weekend-long party. "Come On, Eileen," blared out of one of the windows. Some workers constructed a stage for bands to play on and one dorm already had a keg going. A banner hung along one wall of the quad, proclaiming, 80S BLOWOUT! THE *CURE* FOR WHAT AILS YA.

Britta rolled her eyes. "Theme parties. So lame."

"*She'll* be lame if she doesn't stop sulking," Mads whispered. "I'll break her toes myself."

Lina, Mads, and Holly were bonding already—bonding over how annoying Britta was being. Holly hoped that bringing her along wouldn't turn out to be yet another in her recent, seemingly endless series of mistakes.

They gathered up their overnight bags and trooped up to Piper's suite, which consisted of two double bedrooms and a shared living room. Piper—pretty, thin and dark-haired like Jen—was barefoot in her jeans and blue satin tank top.

"It's a little tight in here, but this is a foldout couch," Piper explained. "So you can sleep two on the couch and two on the floor, in sleeping bags."

"We came prepared," Holly said, tossing two sleeping bags in a corner.

A bleary-eyed girl with a long mane of curly red hair came out of one of the bedrooms. "This is my roommate, Naomi," Piper said. "Just waking up from her disco nap."

"Morning," Naomi said, even though it was five o'clock in the evening. "*Mi casa es su casa.*"

"Thanks," Holly said.

"Jess and Shannon are out somewhere," Piper said. "They both have boyfriends, so you might not see them all weekend. You never know." She scanned their faces. "You're a peppy group. Come on! It's the weekend! Dr. Piper prescribes a campus tour, followed by party after party after party."

Piper led them through the campus, past the rows of frats and sororities, the academic buildings, Hoover Tower and the Main Quad, the Oval, a fountain called the Claw with ducks swimming in it, the student union and Lake Lagunita, where students picnicked, swam, and windsurfed.

"Isn't it gorgeous?" Holly asked Britta.

"Yes," Britta said. "But I already knew that."

"And not just the campus," Mads said, pointing out a clutch of guys in shorts playing touch football.

"Are you applying here next year, Britta?" Piper asked. "You should. I really love it."

"I was thinking about it, before," Britta said. "Now I'm

not sure. Everybody looks so—*California*."

"What's that supposed to mean?" Piper asked. "We're *in* California—how are they supposed to look? *You're* from California . . ."

She glanced at Holly, and the question in her eyes was, *What's with her?*

"Britta might want to go to England for college," Holly said.

The tour ended at the dining hall. Mads loaded up her tray with three kinds of bread, zucchini, roast chicken, salad, and cake. "Mads, you'll never eat all that," Holly said. They settled their trays at a table and went to the soda fountain for drinks. Mads filled three glasses with three different kinds of soda.

"*Mads*," Holly said.

"I know," Mads said. "This is a nightmare for me. I don't handle abundance well."

That's when she noticed the frozen yogurt machine. "Oh my god," she said. "You can have as much frozen yogurt as you want—at every meal? This is some kind of diabolical plot to turn me into a blimp."

"Here's the plan," Piper said. "Naomi and I are making the rounds of the frat parties tonight." She paused. Holly, Mads, and Lina perked up like puppies at a pound hoping to be adopted. Britta picked at her chicken potpie.

"Try not to embarrass me," Piper added. "Just stand in the corner and keep your mouths shut."

"That sounds like a blast," Britta said.

"Or you could spend the whole weekend in the suite," Piper warned. "And we don't have cable."

"Frat party! Frat party!" Mads said.

"Which frat was that again?" Lina asked as they trooped out of one dark, crowded, noisy house and headed into the next one. They were on their fourth party of the night, and all the frat houses looked the same to them.

"I think it was Sigma Chi," Mads said. "That's what some guy told me, anyway."

Britta touched her head. Her curls were limp and damp. "I have beer in my hair," she said.

"Yee haw!" Mads said. "That means you're partying hard."

"No, it means some jerk sprayed beer on me," Britta said.

"Maybe I should drop you guys back at the suite," Piper said. "It's getting late." She glanced at Ben, a friend of hers who'd been hanging around with them most of the night. Holly knew Piper liked him, and it looked like things were heating up between them. No wonder Piper wanted to ditch them.

"No!" Mads protested. "We're having our crazy college weekend!"

"But there are more parties tomorrow," Piper said. "You need to get your beauty sleep, save up your energy, all that stuff."

"I'm ready for bed," Britta said.

"Hey, Piper, you coming?" Ben stood at the threshold of another party, beckoning her.

"I think Piper needs some Ben time," Holly said. "We can find our way back," she told Piper.

"Thanks, Holls," Piper said. "I'll see you girls later. Much later."

Holly, Lina, Mads, and Britta walked back to the suite. It was after midnight, but most of the campus was still wide awake.

"All those houses smelled the same," Britta said. "Like stale beer and smoke. And the floors were sticky."

"And it was so dark I could hardly see anyone's face," Lina said.

"But I still had fun," Mads said. "Even though no one really talked to us or anything."

"That one boy talked to you," Lina said. "The one with the nose ring?"

"He was cute, but I can't get past nose rings," Mads said. "What happens when you have a cold? How do you blow your nose? If I were with a nose ring guy I would never stop thinking about snot."

Lina laughed, and she and Mads chattered away. Holly and Britta fell behind a bit.

"Are you okay, Britta?" Holly asked. "I mean, I know you're upset . . ."

"I'm sorry," Britta said. "I know I'm being a bummer, but I can't help it. I can't stop thinking about my parents. That's what bothers me most of all. How did they find out about my plans with Ed? It's driving me crazy!"

Holly's stomach knotted. The guilt was getting to her.

"I go over and over it in my mind," Britta said. "And the only answer is they totally invaded my privacy. Like, on a criminal level. How could they do that to me? My own parents?"

I should tell her the truth, Holly thought. "They love you," she said. "They care about you. Wouldn't you do the same if you were worried about them?"

"No, I wouldn't," Britta insisted. "It's wrong. Period."

The knot in Holly's stomach tightened. *Face it,* a voice in Holly's head said. *You're chicken.*

Holly couldn't deny it. The truth was going to have to wait.

22 What's He Doing Here?

To:	linaonme
From:	your daily horoscope

HERE IS TODAY'S HOROSCOPE: CANCER: You're waking up, you're smelling the coffee. Finally.

You know what I like about this place?" Lina said. She lounged on a blanket on the shore of Lake Lagunita after lunch on Saturday. Mads and Lina sat beside her, watching Piper play volleyball with some friends. The sun, warm and yellow, beat down on their faces. The blue water sparkled, and windsurfers and sailboats darted like dragonflies over the lake.

"The weather?" Holly guessed.

"The hotties?" Mads said.

"No," Lina said. "Those things are good, though."

"The architecture?" Holly asked.

"The freedom?" Mads said.

"There's no Ramona here," Lina said. "And no Dan. No reminders of all that." Her obsession was fading, and this weekend was helping it melt further and further away. Lina could feel her spirits lifting. She felt as if she'd been living under a damp blanket for the past few months.

"That *is* a good thing," Holly said.

"You know what *I* like best?" Mads asked. "Besides the boys and the fact that my parents and Audrey are a hundred miles away?"

"The frozen yogurt?" Lina said.

"No," Mads said. "Being with you guys. All three of us together. And not being in constant crisis mode."

"I like that, too," Holly said.

Their eyes traveled over to Britta, who was sitting under a tree, furiously scribbling on a pad of paper. "I wonder what she's writing," Mads said. "A letter to Ed?"

"I guess," Holly said. "Or an angry rant."

"I wish she'd relax and have fun," Lina said. "She's making me nervous."

"I think she'll calm down soon," Holly said.

Lina and Mads looked doubtful. Lina closed her eyes and lay back, letting the sun warm her face.

A cell phone buzzed. "Yours, Lina," Mads said. She had a good ear for cell phone rings.

Lina opened her eyes and pulled her cell phone out of her jacket pocket. She read the caller ID and groaned. "Guess who."

"Dr. Syl," Holly guessed. She'd already called three times: once in the car on the way to Palo Alto and twice the night before.

"You win a free trip to Nagsville," Lina said, clicking on her phone. "Hello Mom, everything's fine, don't worry, I haven't become a drug-crazed nymphomaniac yet."

"Lina? I don't like your tone," Sylvia said.

Lina sighed. It was no use upsetting Sylvia; that would only make her call more often. "I'm sorry, Mom. We're sitting outside in the sun. Piper's taking good care of us, and I ate a healthy breakfast *and* lunch. Okay?"

"I don't mean to bother you, Lina," Sylvia said. "I just like to make sure you're all right. Do you have sunscreen on?"

"Yes," Lina lied. "Of course. Do you think I'd leave town without sunscreen?"

"You're getting sassy," Sylvia said. "I don't like that—"

Mads suddenly straightened up. Sylvia talked on while Lina tuned her out.

"Oh my god," Mads said. "That looks just like—"

"I think it is him," Holly said. "That's funny. What would he be doing here?"

"Lina, hang up," Mads said.

"Got to go, Mom. Bye." Lina clicked her phone off and sat up. Across the field a lanky boy with short spiky hair and burnt-butter skin loped toward the lake. Walker. The irritation of talking to her mother faded, replaced by a sudden warm feeling. Lina was glad to see him.

She jumped to her feet. "That's so weird. What's he doing here?"

Without waiting for an answer—and knowing that Mads and Holly didn't have one, anyway—she ran across the grass and intercepted him. "Walker! Hi!" she called.

He stared at her for a second as if trying to remember who she was. He was probably as shocked to see her as she was to see him.

"Lina, hey," he said. "What—are you here for the PSW?"

"The what?" Lina asked. "I'm visiting Holly's sister. Look! Holly and Mads are here, too! And Britta."

Holly and Mads waved.

"That's a funny coincidence," Walker said. "I'm here for a Prospective Students Weekend. It's kind of an early-application thing." Walker was a junior and would be applying to college in the fall. "The university invites some kids to visit for a weekend to see how they like it. I'm staying with a sophomore in East FloMo." At Lina's blank look he added, "It's a dorm on the other side of the Main Quad."

"Oh. Well, listen, what are you doing later?" Lina asked. "Piper's dorm is having a huge party tonight, with a new wave band and everything. It's in Sterling Quad. Want to come?"

Walker stared over her shoulder, toward the lake. "Um, I'm not sure. I've got to see what Kent is doing. That's the guy I'm staying with."

"He can come, too," Lina said. "And bring his friends."

"I'll have to see," Walker said. His voice was cool. Lina suddenly had the feeling he was only being polite to her. He had no intention of coming to the party. "Kent might have other plans."

"Okay. Well, come if you can. It'll be fun."

"All right. See you."

He walked away and joined a group of guys playing Frisbee by the water. Lina returned to the beach blanket. Her warm, happy feeling was gone.

"That was weird," Lina said.

"What did he say?" Mads asked.

"It wasn't what he said, so much," Lina said. "He just acted as if he didn't want to talk to me. As if he didn't like me."

"What?" Holly said.

"It was almost like he was too cool for me," Lina said. "Like he didn't want to be seen with me."

"That's crazy," Holly said. "Walker's not a snob."

"I didn't think so," Lina said.

"Maybe he's just acting weird because he's at a college, with all these older kids," Mads said. "Maybe he doesn't feel comfortable or he's trying to be cool."

"Maybe he's nervous," Holly added.

Lina watched as Walker leaped into the air, caught the Frisbee, and tossed it smoothly to another guy, laughing. "He doesn't look nervous. He looks like he belongs here."

"Maybe he's protecting himself," Holly said.

"From what?" Lina asked.

"From you," Holly said.

"From me? But I'm his friend."

"You've been pretty cold to him, though," Mads said. "You're always blowing him off."

"I am? But we're friends! He understands," Lina said. Then she thought back to that night at Mads' house, making cookies. After the Cleansing Ceremony with Ramona. How she and Mads had missed Holly. The empty feeling she'd had. It was just as easy to hurt a friend as a boyfriend.

Giving up Dan had left a hole in her life. But Walker meant something to her, too. She didn't want to lose his friendship. Why hadn't she seen that before?

If she lost his friendship . . . well, that would make another hole. And how much emptiness could one person take?

23 Declaration of Independence

ead this," Britta said, handing Holly a piece of paper covered with ink. "I'll show my parents they can't run my life!"

The girls had gone back to the suite after the beach barbecue to rest and change. Lina and Mads were napping in one of the bedrooms. Holly sprawled on the couch, and Britta had been sitting at a desk, still furiously working on whatever it was she was writing. Holly took the paper.

Dear Mother and Father,

You have tried to control me my whole life. And I let you. I can't blame myself for this too much—after all, I was just a kid. But now that I am a woman I see how little freedom you've allowed me. After I met Ed, I finally understood who I really am. And that is not just a bookish grind who works like a machine, without emotion, for the empty, soulless goal of getting into a good college. Under your ever-watchful eyes I can't be myself. And I see how corrupt you are. How can I live with people who stoop so low as to read my diary or break into my private e-mail? It's like living in a police state! I have rights just like everybody else—and if you won't respect them, then I must cut my ties with you.

I hereby declare myself independent of you. I plan to file for a legal separation from you. I've already talked to a lawyer about this— maybe you already know that, since you listen in on all my calls. I will be an independent minor, and then you can't stop me from doing what-ever I want! Which in this case is being with Ed. Once I'm independ-ent I can go to England and be with him, whether you like it or not.

I know this hurts you and I'm glad. You brought this on your-selves.

Your former daughter,
Britta

A wave of nausea washed over Holly. She couldn't speak. Britta was cutting off her parents forever—because of the terrible things she *thought* they'd done. But Holly knew they hadn't done anything wrong. Holly had.

She was wracked with guilt. This had gotten way out of control.

Holly found her voice at last. "Britta, you can't do this."

"It's what they deserve," Britta said.

"No, it isn't," Holly said. "You'll break their hearts. And all they've done is love you and worry about you."

"If they really loved me they would let me do what I need to do to be happy," Britta said. "Ed and I *are* getting married. And nobody can stop us."

This can't go on any longer, Holly thought. *I've got to tell Britta the truth.*

"Britta, your parents never spied on you," Holly said.

"Then how did they know where to find me?" Britta stared at her, eyes blazing, waiting to hear what Holly would say next. "How?"

Holly's hands shook. "I told them."

Britta gasped. She said nothing for a whole minute. Holly clutched her stomach, it hurt so much.

"You told them? After I trusted you?" Britta's eyes filled with tears. "After you *promised* you wouldn't?"

"You don't understand," Holly said. "Your mother called me and she was so worried. She was crying! She loves you so much, and she was going to call the police. . . . She was afraid you'd been kidnapped, or dead, and I couldn't let her suffer that way—"

"You couldn't let HER suffer? What about me? I'm the one who's suffered here! Because of you I can't see Ed! Because of you I lost the love of my life! My life is ruined! I have to live like a prisoner at home, my parents monitoring my every move, because of YOU!"

She stood and stomped around the room in rage and frustration. Holly cowered on the couch.

"I thought I could trust you, Holly, but no! Ed is the only person in the whole world I can trust. I never should have left him this weekend to come with you!"

"Britta, I'm sorry!" Holly cried. "I'm so sorry. I was trying to help you!"

"Some friend," Britta snapped. "You're such a hypocrite. A fake! You ask if true love can survive high school? What about this: Can true love survive your so-called friends?"

Britta ran out of the suite, slamming the door. Holly sank her head into her hands. She felt guilty, confused. . . . She had tried so hard to do the right thing. To help Britta. But now Britta was so unhappy. . . . Maybe Holly was wrong. She should have stayed out of it. Never gotten involved. If Britta wanted to be Mrs. Ed Whatever-his-name-was, maybe Holly should have let her. It was Britta's life, after all.

"It's nine o'clock," Holly said. "Where is she?"

Holly, Lina, Mads, and Piper had spent the past hour dressing for the party. Piper immediately vetoed what the younger girls had brought to wear and let them borrow her clothes and makeup. It would have been fun, normally, but Holly couldn't enjoy it. She'd walked all over the campus looking for Britta, but there was no sign of her. Britta had been gone for four hours now. This was getting serious.

"Holly, you're such a prig," Piper said. "Let's go down to the party. I'll bet she's down there already and she's forgotten all about your stupid fight."

Holly stuck her head out the window and looked down into the quad. Music from two competing stereos blasted from windows somewhere in the dorms. Japanese lanterns rimmed the square, the band was setting up on the platform, and people were pouring in through the entrance gate. It was filling up quickly. She couldn't see Britta, but it was dark out there.

Piper put an arm around her. "Stop worrying. This is college. People come and go, they don't tell anyone, they do what they want, they get caught up in a party or a game or something. . . . I mean, what could have happened to her?"

It hit Holly like a thunderbolt. Britta wasn't interested in games and parties. She was interested in one thing: Ed.

"I know what happened to her," Holly said. "She ran off to find Ed. She's going to try to elope again!"

24 Blond Brushcut

| To: | mad4u |
| From: | your daily horoscope |

HERE IS TODAY'S HOROSCOPE: VIRGO: Feeling lightheaded and dizzy? Hate to break it to you, but it's not love. It's not even a crush. It's your diet.

Mads and Lina held hands and pogoed up and down while the band covered a B-52's song. The quad was mobbed with people dancing under the moon and the Japanese lanterns. Lina kept scanning the crowd.

"Do you see him yet?" Mads asked. She knew Lina was hoping Walker would come to the party.

"No," Lina said.

"What about Holly?" Mads asked.

Lina and Mads jumped up together, calling, "Holly!" At the peak of their jump, in the split-second when they could almost see over the heads of the crowd, Mads tried to glimpse Holly or Walker. Too quick. They tried it again. "Holly!"

This time she saw a flash of blond and a hand waving. In a second Holly was at their side. "Dance with us," Mads said.

The song ended and the crowd cheered. "Thank you. We're the Crash," the lead singer announced. "Here comes another B-52's classic, 'Rock Lobster.'"

The three girls danced together, making up their own versions of the shimmy-shake and the frug. Mads could see that Holly's heart wasn't in it, though. She was convinced that Britta had really eloped, and it was all her fault.

Two boys insinuated themselves between the girls until they were a dancing circle of five. One of them, a short guy with a blond brushcut, definitely had his eye on Mads. By the time the next song started, he'd managed to corral her off to himself. His friend, a preppy/slacker type with chin-length red hair and pale eyes, smiled at Lina and Holly. Holly grabbed Lina and shouted into her ear, "I'm going to check the room and see if Britta called or anything." She disappeared.

Lina danced with the red-haired guy for a few songs. Then Mads saw her pull her pulsating cell phone out of her pocket. Lina rolled her eyes. "I'd better take this," she shouted to Mads. "Or Sylvia will send a SWAT team."

She went off to find a quieter spot to talk, and the red-haired guy disappeared in the crowd. Mads and Blond Brushcut danced to new wave classics until sweat soaked their shirts. The band took a break, and Mads and her dance buddy grabbed some water.

"Are you a freshman?" he asked.

Mads shook her head. "I'm visiting for the weekend. Do you know Piper Anderson?"

"Yeah," he said. "She's in my Psych I section. Did you go to high school with her?"

"Sort of," Mads said. "I'm friends with her sister."

Blond Brushcut assessed her. "What are you, sixteen?"

"Fifteen," Mads admitted.

"I thought you looked kind of young, even for a freshman," the boy said. "What's your name?"

"Madison."

"I'm Owen. You're a funky dancer."

"Thanks."

"The band won't be back up for a while," Owen said. "Want to take a walk?"

"Sure."

He led her out of Sterling Quad, down a lamplit path. They found themselves in a plaza with a big fountain. "This is the Claw," Owen said.

"Why is it called the Claw?" Mads asked.

"I don't know," Owen said. "I've only been here for seven months."

"Where are the ducks?" Mads asked. "When I walked past here yesterday there were ducks."

"I guess they go somewhere else to sleep," Owen said. "All the partying students keep them up at night."

They perched on the edge of the fountain. The water splashed behind them. Mads looked up at the sky, saw the moon and the stars, and shivered happily. *I'm at a college, sitting with a college boy. It's late and I can stay out all night if I feel like it!* There was something romantic about it, and exciting. Mads looked at Owen. He was pretty cute. He danced like a hyperactive robot, though. Hmm . . . what would it be like to have a college boyfriend?

"The moonlight looks pretty on your hair," Owen said. "Kind of—kind of like an oil slick."

"An oil slick? Thanks," Mads said.

"No—I mean it's pretty," Owen said.

"You think oil slicks are pretty?"

"Sure. They have those rainbows in them when the light shines on them—that's like your hair."

"You sure wriggled out of that one," Mads said.

Owen laughed. "I really do think it's pretty."

"I believe you," Mads said.

He stretched on arm around her shoulder and pulled her close. She felt nervous—this was a college boy! What was he going to do?

He kissed her. She closed her eyes and tried to relax. She leaned backward a little too far . . . and fell into the fountain, pulling Owen in with her.

She came up for air, soaking wet and laughing. The shock of the water, the shock of the kiss . . . Owen laughed, too, and splashed water in her face. She splashed him back. Then he grabbed her and kissed her again.

"You're cute," he said.

"You're cute, too," Mads said. A breeze kicked up and she felt chilly. All of a sudden she was flooded with guilt. What was she doing? Why was she kissing this guy? And liking it?

She stood up and Owen helped her out of the fountain. They were soaked. Mads smiled at him to keep him from knowing that anything was wrong, but her mind was racing. What about Stephen? And Sean?

"You want to go back to my room and dry off?" Owen asked. "You could take a nice hot shower there—"

"I'd better get back to my friends," Mads said. "It's

getting late." She wondered whether Britta had come back yet. And something told her a hot shower at Owen's dorm was probably not a smart idea.

"That's cool," Owen said. He took her hands. "I had a nice time dancing with you. And swimming."

"Me, too," Mads said.

"If you come up for another visit, let me know," Owen said.

"I will," Mads said.

He leaned forward and kissed her again. Mads couldn't believe it. Why was she doing this? Why did it feel so good? Shouldn't her lips have gotten an electric shock or something?

"Owen," she said as she pulled away. "I should tell you something. Um, I have a boyfriend."

Owen nodded. "That's cool. I've got a girlfriend, too. Back home in Seattle. And I've kind of got another one here, but she split for the weekend."

"Oh." *Huh,* Mads thought. *I guess this is no big deal.*

"Can we kiss some more?" Owen asked.

"I'd like to, I really would," Mads said. "But I've got to go." She started back to Sterling. "See you around."

"See you."

As she squished down the path in her wet shoes, she turned all these new things over in her mind. She kissed another boy. Should she confess to Stephen?

What good would it do? It would only upset him. But what if someone saw her kissing Owen—and decided to tell Stephen? Then what?

She thought about Jane. Maybe it was just as well she'd never gotten through to Sean. How could Mads know what was really going on between Jane and Damien, or Jane and Sean? These love situations were turning out to be more complicated than they seemed.

The Jane and Sean thing is none of my business, she thought. *I'd better stay out of it.* Now that that was settled, she felt better.

She thought about Owen, how he had a girlfriend, or maybe two. She couldn't help laughing. Could true love survive high school? Mads was learning how hard that was. But if this weekend's sneak peek was any indication, it looked as if true love would have an even tougher time surviving college.

25 Found

Piper's suite was empty, and Britta hadn't called.
Holly sat on the couch for a few minutes,
seething with frustration. What should she
do? Should she call the police, or the Fowlers—and risk
making Britta angrier than ever? But what else could she
do? She couldn't just let Britta disappear.

Holly went back to the party to find Mads and Lina.
She didn't want to make this decision alone. She needed
her friends' advice.

The party was louder and more crowded than ever. Holly bumped into Mads, who was all wet for some reason.

"What happened to you?" Holly asked.

"I fell into a fountain," Mads said. "Did you find Britta?"

Holly shook her head. "Let's get Lina and go back to the room."

They wormed their way through the writhing, sweaty mob of dancers. Holly found Lina dancing with the red-haired guy and tapped her on the shoulder. "We're going back to the room," Holly shouted over the music. "Want to come?"

Lina nodded, smiled at the redhead, gave him a little wave, and grabbed Holly's sleeve so she wouldn't lose her in the crowd. They worked their way through the quad. Then Holly tripped over something—someone's big, sneaker-clad foot.

"Ow! Watch it!" a girl snapped. "You stepped on my foot."

Holly looked up. The girl turned around.

"I don't believe it!" Holly cried. "Britta!"

"Holly! Hey, why aren't you dancing?"

This question was not what Holly expected to hear from Britta. She was so stunned she could only stare at her. She seemed to be with a group of five or six college kids, guys and girls, all dancing together.

"Britta, where have you been?" Lina asked.

Holly regained her senses. "What the hell are you doing?" she shouted over the music. "Get over here!" She grabbed Britta by the arm and dragged her through the crowd. Lina and Mads followed.

"Holly—wait!" Britta said. "I really like that song—" She waved to the kids she was with and called, "I had fun! Maybe I'll see you later!"

Holly didn't stop until they reached Piper's suite. She practically threw Britta onto the couch. "Sit down!" she cried.

Lina and Mads stood beside her. All three crossed their arms, waiting for Britta's explanation. "Britta, we've been looking for you for five hours!" Holly said.

"I'm sorry," Britta said. "Were you worried?"

"Yes, we were worried!" Holly said. "Where were you?"

"I had the greatest time!" Britta said. "After I left here—I was pretty mad at you, I guess, but that wore off—I met this girl named Gwen. She was carrying this biology book—the same one I read last summer—and we started talking, and she said she and her friends were going for a sunset hike in the Foothills and asked me if I wanted to go. They showed me all the different trees they have there, and birds, and flowers . . . and when it got dark we went to their dining hall and ate dinner, and then we hung out in their dorm for a while, and then I remembered the party, so we came back here and started dancing. It's been great! I love college!"

Holly, Lina, and Mads just stared at her. "You've been on campus all this time?" Holly finally said. "Hanging out with some girl named Gwen?"

"Well, not just Gwen. There was Jonathan, and Danielle, and Jason—" She paused and looked at Holly. "What did you think I was doing?"

Holly felt uncomfortable. Hadn't Britta practically threatened to run off with Ed just a few hours before? Or had she imagined it? "Um, I'd rather not say."

"Duh! We thought you ran away to find Ed," Mads said. "It was all you ever talked about. You made it sound like you couldn't have fun without him."

Britta looked thoughtful. "I guess I did. I kind of thought that was true. But now I know better." She perked up and added, "Anyway, I figured you knew I was around somewhere, since I left my overnight bag here."

She reached down and lifted her bag off the floor for proof.

Mads laughed. "It was here the whole time?"

Holly slapped her forehead. It had never occurred to

her to check and see if Britta's bag was gone.

"I've been such an idiot," Holly said. "Britta, come with me. I need to talk to you. Alone." She helped Britta to her feet and pulled her into Piper's empty room. Holly shut the door.

"I'm sorry, Holly," Britta said. "I'm sorry I got so angry with you before. Because you were right. College is fantastic! I'd really regret it if I missed it. And I realize now that I shouldn't sacrifice everything for Ed—especially not something that is so important to me."

"Welcome back to the land of the sane," Holly said. "I just wish you'd called my cell and let me know where you were. I was going crazy! I thought you used this trip as another chance to run away."

"You don't have to worry about that anymore," Britta said. "I've changed my mind about all that. I'm not going to get married right now. I still love Ed, but from now on I'm going to slow things down with him. I can't wait to go to college! And who knows, maybe I will go to college in England."

"I'm glad you're not mad at me anymore," Holly said. "I felt so guilty about what I did to you. Next time I will definitely ask your permission before I tell all your secrets to your mother."

Britta laughed. "Wow, thanks. And I'll ask *your*

permission before I run away again."

"That's good. I wouldn't want to have to implant one of those microchips in your arm."

"I think my parents already did, while I was sleeping," Britta said.

26 The Answer Is Maybe

| To: | mad4u |
| From: | your daily horoscope |

HERE IS TODAY'S HOROSCOPE: CAPRICORN: Your life is a huge mess. But if you put enough mousse in your hair and go for the kooky vintage look, you could make it work for you.

I t's hard to come back to cardboard pizza and cold green beans after seeing what a *real* cafeteria looks like." Mads glanced around at the lunchroom and sighed. She and Holly and Lina were having lunch together at school, back from their Stanford weekend. "Should we demand that they install a frozen yogurt machine?"

"What, you don't like the rock-hard ice-cream

sandwiches they keep in the freezer case?" Holly asked. She had just bought one and banged it on the table to show how indestructible it was. "They're perfect when you feel like breaking a window but you can't find a brick."

"Here, give me that." Mads spotted Sean sitting with his back to her at the next table. She took the ice-cream sandwich and heaved it at the back of his head. "Ow!" Sean cried. He turned around, rubbing his head and scowling at Mads.

"Hey, it does work," Mads said.

"What did you do that for?" Sean asked. Then he reached down, picked up the ice-cream sandwich off the floor, and unwrapped it. "Whoa, dessert. Thanks, kid."

"Sean manages to find a bright side to everything," Mads said.

"Mads—why did you do that?" Lina asked.

Mads shrugged. "I felt like getting his attention. I'm experimenting with different methods."

"Well, now you can cross hitting him in the head off your list," Holly said. "There goes my ice-cream sandwich."

"I'll buy you another one," Mads said.

"Did you have fun with Rob last night?" Lina asked Holly.

"Yes," Holly said. "We didn't do much, just watched a movie. But that's okay. He seems more relaxed now that

Ed is safely back in England. Rob and Ed never quite jelled."

"Rob doesn't go for the lovey-dovey stuff, does he?" Mads said.

"Not in that high-drama, *Wuthering Heights* way," Holly said. "It used to bother me, but now I find it kind of refreshing."

"All that drama takes a lot of energy," Lina said.

"I'm not sure how long I could keep it going," Holly said. "Britta got a letter from Ed already. It was written in red ink, and he decorated the borders with little drawings of hearts and flowers."

"Wow. What did he say?"

"He loves her, he misses her, she's the light of his life," Holly said. "She's back in swoonsville. But she's found a way of dealing. She says all great romances thrive in the face of adversity. So being apart from Ed will only make their love stronger."

"Good luck," Mads said.

"Yeah, we'll see about that," Lina said.

"Can true love survive separation? That's the next great question," Holly said.

"Did we ever decide if true love can survive high school?" Lina asked.

"Check El Diario and see," Mads said.

El Diario by Madison Markowitz
Can True Love Survive High School?

That is the question. And here is my answer. True love is delicate. It needs tender loving care, the best conditions, and the tenacity of a pit bull. High school is rough, tough, crazy, full of temptations, hormones, and people who have lost their minds. Can true love survive all that? Maybe. But it won't be easy. If you do manage to make it past graduation, I think you're safe. You've found it. True love.

X-Rating

Will Holly Anderson, Madison Markowitz, and Lina Ozu please report to Mr. Alvarado's office immediately." The library intercom crackled to life with the sound of the school secretary's nasal voice.

Mads looked at Holly and Lina. "Uh-oh. What *now?*"

"I can't think of anything we've done wrong," Lina said. "We didn't put any of the dirty letters we received on our Web site."

Like the one by the girl who said her ex-boyfriend liked to do it in the car—and only in the car, Mads thought. They knew enough not to put that on the blog. But could something have slipped through the cracks?

"Hello, girls," Rod said at few minutes later in his office. "I've been seeing a lot of you these days."

"If you'd rather not, we can always leave," Mads joked.

Rod cracked a tense smile. "I wish it were that simple. Do you recall the warning I gave you the last time we met?"

The girls nodded. Nothing controversial on the Dating Game or he'd shut it down.

"Good," Rod said. "Did you understand it? Was it somehow not clear?"

"We understood," Mads said. "But maybe we have a different definition of 'controversial' from yours."

"I'm sure you must," Rod said. "Otherwise, I assume an item like this would not have appeared on your blog." He picked up a printout. "I believe this is what you call an X-Rating." He waved the paper in front of them. "I found it in that section where students write in about ex-girl-friends and ex-boyfriends," he said. "A young man named Dashiell Piasecki wrote about his former girlfriend, Arabella Caslow. I happen to know Dashiell; he's a frequent visitor to this office."

Mads tried to remember what Dash had written about Arabella. He was an obnoxious jerk, and Arabella had said so in *her* X-Rating of *him*. But his of her hadn't seemed so bad; in fact, Mads had the impression he still liked her.

"I'll skip the preliminaries and go straight to the high-lights," Rod said. He read from the printout. "'Arabella is a bangin' chick.'"

"Mr. Alvarado, all he's saying is that Arabella is pretty," Holly explained. "It's a *good* thing."

"That's not the point," Rod said. "Her parents happened to see this—I should warn you that since you've received so much publicity recently, many parents have been reading our school site quite carefully. The Caslows were offended by the word bangin' in reference to their daughter."

"Bangin' just means she's good-looking," Mads said.

"But in a sexy way, correct?" Rod said.

"I guess," Mads conceded.

"Was Arabella herself upset?" Lina asked.

"I don't know," Rod said. "But her parents certainly were. They don't like having their daughter's attributes discussed online this way, and I don't blame them. It's crude."

"But Dash was just trying to say she'd make a good girlfriend," Mads explained. "Sure he's crude, but that's the way he is. It's not our fault."

"Listen, girls," Rod said. "I refuse to get into an argument with you over this. You were warned, fair and square. Since then, the complaints from parents have only grown louder. I have no choice. I'm removing the Dating Game from the school site. I'm sorry."

"But Mr. Alvarado, that's not fair!" Mads' blood was boiling. He was dumping their blog completely! "What good is the site, if we can't express ourselves naturally and say what we really think in the words we normally use? It's—"

Rod cut her off. "Enough. I said I won't argue about it. This is the way it is, period. Please leave my office now." He started shuffling papers around on his desk as if he were busy. Mads got up and left, followed by Holly and Lina.

"I can't believe it!" Mads cried, once they were out in the hall. "What are we going to do now?"

"We could move the Dating Game to a site of our own," Lina suggested.

"Or one of those blog sites like Autumn uses," Holly said.

Mads stamped her foot. "No. It's not right. It's the principle of the thing. The Dating Game was a special RSAGE feature. It was only open to us and protected from infiltration by anyone outside the school. It was part of the school community. It brought us all together, gave us a common place to say what's on our minds. That's what was cool about it. And anyway, this is totally unfair. We can't let Rod and those control-freak parents do this to us! We may be kids, but we have rights!"

Holly and Lina stared at her with their jaws hanging open. "Wow, Mads, you're really fired up. I've never seen you like this," Lina said.

"Well, there are things we can do," Mads said. "We're not beaten yet."

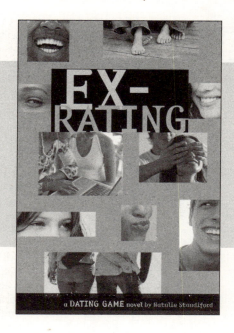

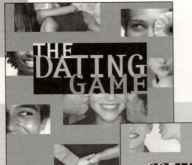
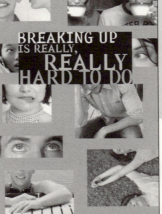